AN APPLE FOR MISS DELANEY

AN APPLE FOR MISS DELANEY

•

Mike Gaherty

AVALON BOOKS
THOMAS BOUREGY AND COMPANY, INC.
401 LAFAYETTE STREET
NEW YORK, NEW YORK 10003

© Copyright 1998 by Mike Gaherty
Library of Congress Catalog Card Number 98-96070
ISBN 0-8034-9296-0

PRINTED IN THE UNITED STATES OF AMERICA
ON ACID-FREE PAPER
BY HADDON CRAFTSMEN, BLOOMSBURG, PENNSYLVANIA

In loving memory of my sister Helen,
who always loved the mountains.

Chapter One

The secretary opened the door, directed Heather DeLaney to a chair, and left. Heather sat uncomfortably and squinted her eyes against the brilliant background of the wall of windows, the afternoon sun being in perfect position to blind her. When her eyes adjusted a little to the glare, she could make out a row of five tablet-arm desks facing her and occupied by her interviewers. She raised her hand to shield her eyes, and a man whom she recognized as the superintendent, Dr. Shoemaker, struggled out of his undersized chair. She'd met him just this morning in his office. He seemed like a pleasant enough sort, she had decided at the time. She guessed him to be about fifty. He was a little on the paunchy side, with a heavy-jowled face to match his size. His receding hairline had just about caught up with the bald spot in the back.

He smiled as he passed in front of her. "I'm sorry. Let me adjust those blinds." He moved to the wall of windows. "It looks like some kind of interrogation, doesn't it? I assure you we're all friends here."

As he flipped the blinds up, the others lined before her came into better focus. As she scanned their somber faces, she wasn't so sure about Dr. Shoemaker's *friends* remark. The superintendent made his way back to his place and squeezed into the chair. "Now, that's better, isn't it?" He smiled and Heather nodded. "Now then, let's get started, shall we?" He tried to cross his legs but banged a knee against the tablet arm. "I'm getting too old for these blasted desks," he said in a grumble. "Don't we have any real chairs?"

A thin, middle-aged, pinched-faced woman, who Heather

guessed to be the elementary principal, turned a forced smile on the superintendent from her place at one end of the line. "I can have one brought in from the main office for you."

Dr. Shoemaker waved a hand at her. "No, no, I'll manage."

"We could have met in my office, but it would have been cramped. Or your office at administration, but you said . . ."

"I know what I said, Miss Nordway. This will be fine. Let's get on with it."

Yes, what a happy group, Heather thought to herself. As her gaze passed over the five faces before her, she found herself focusing on one person who seemed somehow out of place. Maybe it was something about the rigid set of his mouth that suggested he was out of step with these proceedings. His face, lean and angular and tanned, was accented by a neatly trimmed, small, reddish beard. The beard contrasted in color with his hair, which was dark and carelessly wavy, kept just short enough to be manageable.

As she tried to guess the color of his eyes, which struck her as dark and brooding, he looked up from the folder he had been studying and stared directly at her. She held his gaze just long enough to see what appeared to her to be a definitely hostile look in his eyes. *Now what's that all about?* she thought, as she glanced away. *What's this guy's problem?* She could still feel those dark eyes boring into her, and though she struggled to fight it, she knew the color was rising to her cheeks. *This is not the way to start a job interview,* she warned herself, but, ignoring her own warning, she stared back and set her jaw. Finally he looked away. *Feel better now?* she asked herself, knowing only too well that such social gamesmanship could tip the scales against her. Just then she became aware that the superintendent was talking, and for how long she hadn't a clue.

". . . of involving various elements of the school community in the hiring process. At my far right is Janis Nordway, the principal of Keats Elementary." The principal offered Heather a weak, forced smile. "And next to her is Mary Lane, one of our fourth-grade teachers." Heather felt definite empathy in the look she received from this young, attractive woman. Mary Lane had been through this same ordeal herself just two years earlier at the start of her teaching career, and she knew exactly what Heather was going through.

The superintendent continued. ''And to my left here is our personnel director, Amy Bodaker. You two have talked on the phone, I believe.'' Both women nodded. ''Miss Bodaker was out of the office this morning when you stopped by.'' Heather was shocked at the other's appearance. She didn't match her gentle, soothing, songlike telephone voice. *Rugged* was what came to Heather's mind to describe the woman. She was stocky and leathery from too much sun exposure. *I'll bet she hikes and camps and skis and everything,* Heather thought. Her age was impossible to guess. Her smile was genuine and definitely friendly, though. Heather began to relax ever so slightly. *Maybe this won't be so bad,* she allowed herself to think.

''We always try to include at least one parent in our job interviews. We're happy Marc Adams has agreed to join us.'' The superintendent nodded toward the man at the end of the row. ''He's something of a celebrity around town, a nationally recognized artist. His paintings hang in homes and galleries around the world.''

Her interest heightened, Heather looked from the principal's face to this Marc Adams, only to be met by the same stare that had stopped her dead a minute ago. Yes, his eyes were definitely brown, a very dark brown, and they were now boring right through her again. The feeling of comfort she had been enjoying only a moment ago was gone. She looked away again, but this time more slowly.

''Let me explain how this process works,'' Dr. Shoemaker continued. ''First, we'll ask you to tell us something about yourself, your accomplishments, your education, your philosophy of teaching—anything you think is pertinent. It's up to you. Then we'll open it up for questions from the committee here. Does that meet with everyone's approval?'' He glanced quickly down the row and then at Heather. ''Okay, Miss DeLaney, do you want to start things off?''

Heather was still trying to fathom the hostile look she was getting from this Marc Adams. She felt a reluctance to turn toward him because she just knew his eyes were still burning into her. As she opened a folder she'd been holding on her lap, a slight tremor shook the pieces of paper. She struggled to control her hands, and then a hot anger started to grow inside her. *I don't know what's going on with this guy, but he's not going to get the better of me. So he's a nationally recognized artist. Big deal. I'm the best teacher this committee is going to see.* She raised her head confidently, a look of haughtiness replacing her earlier insecurity.

Marc Adams had been studying Heather DeLaney carefully from the moment she entered the room. *How come the teachers I had in school never looked like that?* he wondered. He especially noticed her delicate features. *She's smart enough not to mess up a perfect complexion with a lot of makeup like some women do. That skin tone would be hard to duplicate. Hard to match that pink in her cheeks. I'll bet she burns if she even thinks about the sun. She doesn't look like she sits in the house all day, though. Not like Bodaker, that's for sure, but who needs a woman who looks like she lives on the bank of a river or something? I bet she runs or plays golf or something. Probably skis. Yeah, that's why she wants to come here, I bet.* As Heather turned her head to avoid the sun coming through the blinds, he saw the highlights given off by her deep brown hair done up neatly in the back. *What do they call that? French braid? I think that's what it is. How long does it take a woman to get her hair to look like that every day?*

He glanced down at the folder in front of him. *Twenty-six years old. Three years with Denver public schools. So she's coming down from Mt. Olympus, bringing the enlightened word to us poor mountain folk.* He glanced up from the folder and caught her staring at him. He met her gaze until she looked away. She looked back and he turned his attention to the bio on his desk. *Feisty little thing, aren't you?* he thought. The superintendent's flat voice droned in the stuffy room. *Old Gene loves to hear himself talk.* He heard his own name mentioned in glowing terms and caught the look of curiosity in Miss DeLaney's eyes as she turned toward him. He stared back coldly. *Yes, you heard right, Miss Denver Public Schools. I'm the famous art has-been at the ripe old age of thirty-two.* He watched the proud tilt of her head as she began talking and knew he had tabbed her right. *She has all the answers to whatever we're supposedly doing wrong,* he thought.

By sheer force of will, Heather commanded herself to keep her hands steady and to speak in a firm, controlled voice. "I am originally from St. Louis, Missouri. My parents still live there with my younger brother. He's going to be a senior in high school this fall. I fell in love with this area when I was just a kid on vacations with my family. My dad tried skiing a long time ago and fell for it hard, which is pretty tough when you're a flat-lander." She got some smiles from her audience with this. "So we came out here to Bear Claw a couple of times every winter. My dad used to sneak away more often than that. So when it came time to go to college, I decided to get a little closer to the mountains and went to CU at Boulder.

"I always liked working with little kids. I did my thing as a camp counselor in high school, and I volunteered as an aide for a preschool, so I always knew I wanted to be a teacher. At CU I got involved in a special program for accelerated kids and was hired to establish a pilot program for the gifted in the Denver public schools. I've taught there for the last three years. I heard about an opening here from my cousin, who lives here in Keats. Maybe you know her? Jessie Tompkins?"

Miss Nordway beamed. "Why, yes. Both Mr. and Mrs. Tomp-kins have been very involved here at school."

"Is that Jerry Tompkins at Crossridge State Bank?" Dr. Shoe-maker asked.

"That's right. And Jessie works part-time at the West Wind Gallery." Heather turned her head slightly and glanced at Marc Adams for the first time in several minutes. "Maybe you know her, Mr. Adams?"

"No," he said flatly, still staring through her with those dark eyes.

Well, excuse me for trying to be friendly, Heather said to her-self. She stared at the folder in her hand and stammered ever so slightly. "Well, I guess that's about all. You have my involve-ment in organizations in front of you. I'd just like to finish by saying I'd love to teach here. As I said, I've been coming to

Keats since I was a little girl, and I've always dreamed of living here in the mountains.''

''And that dream of yours,'' broke in Marc Adams suddenly, ''that did involve something more than playing on the ski slopes? You were planning to squeeze in some teaching too, weren't you?'' His voice was dripping with sarcasm.

Heather's face reddened slightly, and she shifted in her chair. ''Of course, Mr. Adams. That goes without saying.''

Dr. Shoemaker recovered from his shock at Marc Adams's rude comment. ''Yes, well, now I guess that does lead us into the question-and-answer segment. Are there other questions from the committee?''

''I've got a couple more.'' It was Marc Adams again. ''It's August and you're job hunting. What happened? Did you get fired by Denver?''

''No, of course not,'' Heather shot back at him indignantly. ''As a matter of fact I'm still under contract. Because of the financial crunch the Denver public schools are facing, the funding for the program I've been working with was cut just two weeks ago. I've been reassigned as a permanent sub until a regular position opens up.''

Mr. Adams wasn't letting up. He was slouched slightly in his chair now, slapping the closed folder on the tablet arm. ''Permanent sub, huh? So you don't want to get your hands dirty down in the trenches.''

Dr. Shoemaker tried to interrupt, but Heather DeLaney was more than ready to defend herself. She was angry with this man and his insinuations. ''I've been in the trenches, as you call it, for three years, Mr. Adams, but for your information I don't relish the insecurity of being a sub. I want my own classroom.''

''What you mean is that you want a classroom where you can foist a defunct experimental program on the kids at Keats Elementary,'' Mr. Adams snapped. He was becoming unreasonable and even he knew it.

''No, I have no intention of foisting anything on this school system if I'm hired. I expect to abide by the course of study set up by the district.''

Marc Adams suddenly sat up and leaned out over the tablet arm in front of him. ''You expect us to believe that? You'll be trying the latest education mumbo jumbo on our kids as soon as our backs are turned."

"Here now!" interrupted the superintendent.

Heather ignored him. She felt the heat of anger building inside. "I repeat that I would follow the program outlined by this district, but I certainly disagree with your term *mumbo jumbo* to categorize anything new in the field of education."

Marc Adams was staring through her again, but if he thought he was going to force her to look away, he was badly mistaken. In fact there was such fire in her eyes, he felt it necessary to drop back in his chair, and then slouched as before, almost defensively. She had stood up to his unreasonable bluster, and everyone in the room knew it. "You think you've got all the answers, don't you?" he said, sounding for all the world like a child wanting the last word.

Heather let out an exasperated breath of air. She had no intention of granting him that last word, but before she could respond, Dr. Shoemaker interrupted again, this time with a firm resolve to gain control of the meeting. "This has gone about far enough. Miss DeLaney, could I please ask you to step outside for just a moment? I'm terribly sorry." Heather did as she was told, though she was more than ready to answer the charges of this rude and poorly informed man.

Dr. Shoemaker waited until the door had closed behind her before he turned on Marc Adams. "Marc, what in heaven's name are you trying to do? This is supposed to be a simple hiring review committee. It's not supposed to be some kind of a criminal trial. This young woman comes to us with excellent credentials. You act like you've got some kind of personal vendetta against her."

Marc knew well enough that he had gone too far, but something about this DeLaney woman had just set him off. She looked so sure of herself. He didn't trust people who looked like they had all the answers. And he had such a habit of judging people by some silly first reaction. He always seemed to do that. He never should have agreed to be a part of this group in the first place. His place was in his studio with his painting, where he belonged. It was obvious he couldn't tolerate the company of others even for such a simple thing as a school committee. Hadn't he told Gene he didn't want to do it? He shouldn't have let the old windbag talk him into this.

He stood suddenly and tossed the bio folder on Miss Bodaker's desk, much to her surprise. "Okay," he said petulantly, "if you want to hire some outsider to come in and ruin our kids, you can do it without me." Even as he said it, he realized how ridiculous his accusation was, but he wasn't going to take it back now. He headed for the door while the other four exchanged rolled-eye glances. He yanked open the door and burst out into the hall and, in his haste to escape, nearly ran into Heather, who was pacing angrily outside. He glared at her without so much as a word and strode for the front door. "Well, excuse you," she said after him to claim the last word, but whether he had not heard her or pretended not to hear her, it was impossible to tell. "Good riddance," she said more to herself than to anyone else, but when she turned she nearly collided with Dr. Shoemaker, who had stepped out of the room to invite her back.

If he heard her parting words, he didn't let on. "Miss DeLaney, shall we begin again?" he asked with exaggerated gentleness.

Chapter Two

Heather relaxed on Jess and Jerry's redwood deck. She took a sip of lemonade and leaned back, taking in the panorama in front of her. The mountains looked especially majestic, highlighted as they were by the afternoon sun. But they were always majestic to her. She wondered if she would ever tire of seeing them. Now that she was to become a permanent resident, would she go about her daily routine and forget to look up at them? She hoped not. She sought out Big Bear Mountain, the tallest of the dozen or so peaks she could see from where she sat. She could still see two snow patches high on its slope even this late in the season. And now in the next couple of weeks, dustings of snow at those higher elevations would signal the change of seasons, and she was going to be a part of it all. She shivered with excitement.

Heather's cousin Jess appeared at the screen door. "I just can't get over it. You got the job! I'm so excited. Now I'll be out there in two minutes to hear every detail. Just give me time to stick the roast in the oven."

Heather started out of her deck chair. "Here, let me help. Can I peel potatoes or something?"

"You stay right where you are. I'm almost done."

"You're spoiling me," Heather shouted, but Jess was already digging through the freezer and didn't hear.

A moment later she slid the screen door open and stepped out onto the deck. Heather watched her cousin with a smile. She never ceased to marvel at the energy of this woman. Jess would have to stand on tiptoe to measure five feet tall, and if she weighed a hundred pounds it was because she was holding their

9

cat, Mitzi, with her on the scale. But she could go from early morning to late at night nonstop. Heather really hadn't gotten to know this cousin of hers, her mother's niece, until coming west for college. They'd both grown up in St. Louis, but Jess was ten years older, and, as they were growing up, those ten years had created a mighty gulf between the two. But no longer. Now they were more like sisters than cousins.

"So tell me everything," Jess said excitedly as she dropped into a deck chair. "Don't leave out a syllable. Did you expect them to offer you the job today? I didn't think that's the way it was done."

"Same here, but I had some help from a parent. A Mr. Marc Adams."

Jess's jaw dropped. "Marc Adams? What in the world would he have to do with hiring you?"

Heather described the exchange between the two in great detail. "So when Dr. Shoemaker called me back into the room, the committee asked me a few powder-puff questions and then offered me the job. Just as simple as that. I know they must have been impressed with the way I stood up to that ogre." She took a long swig of her lemonade. "So I guess I owe it all to Mr. Adams." Her tone changed as she looked at Jess with her brow knitted. "What is wrong with that man, anyway? He was horrible. I pity his poor wife."

Jess shook her head slowly and clicked her tongue. "There is no wife. And that's the problem. She and their baby daughter were killed when her car was run off a road just outside of town by a drunk driver. It was just awful. Everybody says he's had a total personality change since it happened."

Heather felt a sinking feeling in her stomach. She was already feeling sorry for the thoughts that had been running around in her head about the man. "That's just terrible. When did it happen?"

Jess stared up at the sky in thought. "Hm, must be about two years now." She scrunched up her face. "Let's see, it was just after school started, from what I remember. That's why their little boy wasn't with her. I'm pretty sure it will be two years this fall. People are thinking he should be snapping out of it."

"That's quite a bit for anyone to get over."

"Apparently so. Before the accident he was involved in everything around town. Since then he's just pulled away. I don't really know him, but I know some people who do. In fact, a good friend of mine works in his studio part-time. She says people just try to stay out of his way.''

''What about the little boy?''

''That little boy is the center of Marc Adams's universe now, from what I hear. His name's Jason. Rumor has it that he's having some trouble in school. But is that any wonder? He was old enough to know what was going on when his mother was killed, and I'll bet the dad isn't helping matters, the way he acts. Poor kid.''

The two sat in silence. Heather watched the afternoon clouds begin to build behind the peaks in the distance. It was her ability to empathize with the problems of others that made her such a good teacher. But it wasn't something she could turn on and off. And often the misfortunes of others, tied to her even remotely, could darken her own mood.

''But you got the job.'' Jess had broken the silence and was intent on restoring a note of celebration. ''That's wonderful. It will be great having you so close. And I'll bet we'll see more of your mom and dad with you in town.''

Heather came back from her thoughts reluctantly. ''Right. It is wonderful.'' But the tone of her voice was much subdued. ''Oh, yeah, Dad will be pleased. Knowing him, he'll be camped out at my place, waiting for ski season. And speaking of a place, I've got to start looking.''

''That's the one bad thing about this town. It's not easy to find something. Unless you're a movie star with money hanging out of your pockets. But you're coming at a good time. The summer season is winding down, and it will be a good two months before we think about skiing. Everyone in the shops downtown is dying for that little break. We love to see our tourists come, but we love to see them go.''

''So that's what you've been thinking about us all these years.'' Heather laughed.

Jess giggled in the high-pitched way that Heather loved so much. ''Would I think that about our tourist friends? Hey, listen, now you're one of us. What do you care? Now remember, Jerry and I want you to stay right here until you find the perfect place.''

"Thanks, Jess, I appreciate that. I thought I'd commute back to Denver on the weekends if I don't find something by the time school starts. I'll hang on to my apartment there until I find something here. I'd better get back tomorrow afternoon to turn in my resignation. It's kind of late, but what can they expect, the way they pulled the rug out from under me."

"I guess so!" Jess leaned over and put a hand on Heather's arm. "I know you're going to love it here."

Heather smiled and leaned back in her chair. She was beginning to recover some of her feeling of excitement. She gazed toward the sky and was surprised to see that the advancing clouds had already hidden the sun. She felt a cold drop of rain splash just above her right eye, and by the time the two women gathered up their things and hurried inside, the afternoon shower had hidden the distant mountains from view.

Chapter Three

Marc Adams sat staring at his easel. The dark colors sprawled on the canvas stared back at him, mocking him, daring him to add a splash of highlight, a bold red or yellow, anything that would bring life to the drab abstract. He'd tried before to lift his paintings out of the pit of despair and failed. And he'd fail again with this one. Hadn't he been pouring the pain inside him onto this very canvas for three weeks now? And to what avail? It was as depressing and lifeless as its creator.

He was working in the loft studio of his downtown gallery. He kept a studio there and in his home, but he hadn't worked at home for two years now, not since that awful phone call on a Friday interrupted the reverie between artist and canvas with the news that would forever change his life. That painting still rested on its easel, unfinished, a tribute to the artist as he once was. It wasn't that he hadn't tried. He had sat in front of it for hours at a time, trying to rekindle the flight of fancy that would allow him free rein to play with the reds and yellows and blues and greens that the painting required. His grandmother's garden, maybe not as it really was, but as it was filtered through the love and happiness of another time.

The whir of the potter's wheel broke his concentration, and he looked away from the easel to a far corner of the loft, where his son, Jason, sat on a high stool, leaning awkwardly over the wheel, his stubby gray-stained fingers shaping a slender gray column. Marc smiled. Here was the color in his life. The reds and greens and blues and yellows all rolled into one freckle-faced, pint-sized, bright-eyed boy. With a shock of red hair thrown in for good measure.

He watched as the boy, tongue clamped between front teeth, struggled with too-small hands to maneuver the glob of clay into the desired shape. *He's got his mother's talent,* Marc thought. Carole had used that same wheel to turn out some of the most beautiful pottery he had ever seen. She had displayed some pieces in their own gallery, but most in the co-op next door. Carole had allowed Jason to play on the wheel, but now in the last year it was more than just play. He was doing some surprising work for a nine-year-old. Marc had watched kids play on the wheel. Any he had seen lacked the coordination or the control or whatever to create anything worth a second look. But not Jason. He had a certain touch. Oh, still immature and unrefined, to be sure, but he had something special. Marc was sure of it. Why, just this summer he had asked Rene next door to show a few of the boy's pieces, and last week one had sold. Marc hadn't seen him so excited in ages.

Marc's proud smile dimmed. *Is this what a nine-year-old should be doing during his summer vacation?* he wondered. They lived too far up in the mountains for normal vacant-lot neighborhood games. *As if you could find a vacant lot in Keats anyway,* he thought to himself. He scratched his temple with the handle of the brush he was still holding. *Jason doesn't have any school friends to carry over into the summer.* He sighed heavily when he reminded himself of school. *It won't be long,* he thought. The last two years had been a nightmare. Crying at night. Threats of running away. And Jason had loved school before the accident. He set the brush and palette down. *This year is going to be different,* he promised himself. *Maybe I need to do more with him. Get him away from the same setting.*

"Hey, Jason," he shouted across the room. The boy jerked his head in his dad's direction, and the delicate cylinder of clay he was working took a sudden nosedive.

"Aw, Dad, look what you made me do!"

Marc smiled. "Sorry about that, buddy. Hey, I was wondering, what say we knock off early this afternoon and see if we can snag some trout in Cub Creek?"

Marc could see the boy's look from clear across the room. "Dad, you always say the same thing, but we never catch anything."

"Well, I just have a feeling our luck is going to change. Are you with me?"

"All right, but I know there aren't any fish in that stupid river."

"I wouldn't be so sure, but even if we don't catch anything, it's fun looking at the mountains and listening to the river, don't you think?"

"I guess."

A faint bell announced a customer, but Doris was downstairs to handle the tourist trade. Doris Clayborne alternated with Becky Spooner during the week to mind the gallery. Marc dropped in nearly every afternoon to work for a while in the loft, and when he wasn't there, the women could always reach him quickly on his cell phone. Plus, the two women were only too happy to look after Jason at the gallery if Marc had to be somewhere, which wasn't very often.

Marc heard a deep voice roll up from down below. He looked over the railing and saw the bald pate of Arnold McCumber gleaming back at him. "Hey, Arnold, come on up," he called over the railing. A moment later Arnold's heavy tread echoed through the back of the gallery as he made his way up the stairs. Arnold McCumber was a humorless, no-nonsense, fiftyish man who had served as Marc's business manager for nearly ten years. He handled Marc's finances generally and pushed the showings and sales of Marc's paintings outside the gallery, as he did for a handful of the other artists living and working in Keats. And Marc knew he was good at what he did. He was an extremely tall, cadaverous fellow who walked slowly, with a slight stoop of the shoulders. He nodded solemnly at Jason in the corner and came to stand behind Marc. He surveyed the canvas for a long moment. "Hm. More of the same, I see."

"And a good afternoon to you too," Marc snapped.

Arnold cast a quick look at Jason. "Marc, we need to talk." He looked nervously over at the boy again.

"Okay, okay, I get the point. Jace, how about taking a break? I need a yogurt. Run get us a couple of cones at TCBY? You know what I want. You want something, Arnold?"

"No, nothing for me, thanks."

Jason was poking a finger in the mound of clay on the wheel.

"Chocolate and vanilla swirl, Dad? Like always?" He hopped down from his stool and came to stand by his dad, waiting for the money. He looked up into Arnold's face. "How long am I supposed to be gone, Mr. McCumber?"

Marc chuckled as he handed over the bills. "Don't get smart, buddy. And wipe off those hands before you touch my cone." The boy ran back to the wheel and made a quick rub of his hands with an old towel before he headed for the stairs.

"Mighty perceptive little guy," Arnold remarked when he heard Jason skip down the steps.

"Well, he's not stupid. You're about as subtle as a mafia hit man when a nine-year-old can see through you. So what's on your mind that's so hush-hush?"

Arnold took a deep breath to prepare himself for what he knew was going to be ugly business. "Marc, I hate to have to be the one to tell you this, but somebody has to. Something's got to be done about your painting."

"What about my painting?" Marc twisted in his director's chair and fixed Arnold with one of his patented stares.

"It's depressing. It's morbid. I'm having a hard time even placing it in galleries."

"Don't try to sugarcoat it," Marc said sarcastically. "Give it to me straight. I can take it."

"Well, you asked, so I told you."

"Thanks so much. Since when did you become an art critic, anyway? You wouldn't know a Picasso from a Grandma Moses."

"Who needs to? All I do is watch the cash flow. If the money doesn't come in, something's wrong."

Marc shook his head slowly. "I guess you can't get much more commercial than that. What happened to art for art's sake?"

"C'mon, Marc, don't give me that stuff. I know enough to know your paintings used to be good. They were fun to look at, to hang on your wall. They had lots of color and feeling. People liked what you did with the mountains. You're really good when you're working at that kind of stuff. But you don't do it anymore. All you do is this . . . this abstract business." He pointed toward the painting Marc was working on. "You haven't done anything but this since, well, since . . ." He hesitated. "Well, you know."

"Go ahead and say it, why don't you? Since my wife and baby

daughter were killed in a car accident? Yeah, you're right. Everything changed then.''

"But that's been two years ago, Marc," Arnold pleaded. "Shouldn't you be getting over it?"

Marc rested his forehead in the palm of one hand. "Believe me, Arnold, I try. Sometimes it's all I can do to get out of bed and go through the motions. If it wasn't for that little guy of mine, I don't think I could make it."

The two men said nothing for a long moment. Arnold was wringing his hands in front of him. "I don't know what to say. I wish I could say something that would make things all better, but I can't. Maybe you need to get professional help."

"You mean like a shrink?"

"Well, maybe, but don't they have people who help with grief counseling? It can't be good for your boy."

"You're probably right. I just don't know."

"Well, I know one thing," Arnold said. "It's affected your painting. Take what you're working on here. It looks like every painting you have hanging downstairs. What you're selling is because of your name. But that can't go on forever."

Marc looked up and smiled weakly. "You don't think we could call this my blue period?"

"Hey," Arnold replied evenly, as if any attempt at humor were lost on him, "I don't think that's what they mean by a blue period."

Chapter Four

Heather had the house to herself. Jerry was off at work, and Jess had left with the kids, Tim and Ellen, to buy school clothes. Heather was asked along, but she begged off. This morning she would at least start apartment hunting. And then it was off to Denver in the afternoon to take care of the little matter of a resignation. She'd been studying the apartment listings in the paper over cereal and toast, circling the ones that sounded promising. She called on three, and her first appointment was for ten-thirty. She'd just have time for a run if she hurried. She slipped the dishes in the dishwasher and settled on the living room floor for ten minutes of stretching, a habit she never neglected before running. She threw a towel over her shoulder and headed for her car in the driveway. She stopped herself just before she climbed in. *Almost forgot already*, she thought. She took a deep breath and did a slow three-hundred-and-sixty-degree turn, taking in the mountain view that surrounded her. It was a perfectly gorgeous day—no clouds, and the sky the deepest blue she could ever imagine.

Heather had been coming to Keats long enough to know her way around the town. There was a jogging trail that circled a public park not far from Jess and Jerry's house. She'd run there before and knew it would be perfect for a light workout. She parked her car, did a half-dozen deep knee bends for good measure, and started off at a leisurely clip around what she judged was probably a half-mile circuit that passed through a stand of heavenly scented pines, along a grouping of slides and swings and teeter-totters, already crowded with noisy youngsters, and next to a grassy field with a soccer net at one end and a football

18

goalpost at the other. As she passed the first time, she smiled to herself imagining the problems that could arise over the forced mixing of the two sports.

She made three fairly easy trips around the track for what she guessed would be about a mile and a half. Midway through the fourth circuit, she slowed to a fast walk. It would take her some time to get her body accustomed to this elevation. At seventy-five hundred feet, Keats was more than two thousand feet above Denver, and that was enough to make even a well-trained athlete notice the thin air.

As she rounded a clump of lilac bushes behind the football goalposts, she saw a handful of high-school-age boys trotting onto the field, their voices and laughter filling the morning air. One of the boys streaked for the goalposts, holding his hands in front of him, signaling for a pass. A tall, well-built boy, who had been tossing a football from one hand to the other as he walked, suddenly stepped back two or three paces and spiraled a perfect throw into the outstretched hands. The receiver trotted triumphantly beneath the goalpost. ''How come you can't do that in a game?'' one of the others shouted, bringing a smile to Heather's face.

As she passed the group, now busy breaking into two teams, she caught sight of a little boy, maybe nine or ten, running across the path from a car parked about thirty feet ahead of her, a big black Labrador romping at his side. This boy too had been watching the big boys, because he ran with his hands raised above his head, looking behind him as he had seen the other boy do. A man, Heather assumed it was his father, ran after the boy, a pint-sized football clutched easily in his hand. As he passed in front of her, only twenty feet ahead, she recognized him and quickly reached for the towel draped around her neck, pulling it up so it hung like a scarf over her head. The man was Marc Adams.

She was in no mood to deal with him again, not after yesterday, and she ran the short distance to her car, unlocked the door quickly, and slipped inside. As she closed the door after her, she pulled the towel off her head and sat back to watch the father and son and their dog through the windshield. It took less than thirty seconds to see that Mr. Adams was a different person with his son. *Thank goodness for that*, she thought. She watched as the boy tucked the football under his arm in obvious imitation of players he had seen on television or, for all she knew, at real games. He ran toward some goal the two had already agreed upon, his bright red hair flying, his short legs churning to carry him past his father. Heather smiled as she watched the father feign an attempt to catch the boy, leaping through the air only to come up short as the son scampered laughingly past the out-stretched hands. The big dog, barking in excitement, circled the boy, who was doing some kind of end-zone dance, from what Heather could figure out. At any rate, she couldn't help but laugh at his antics. She could hear the dog's barking from inside the car. She started her car and backed away from the curb. *At least he's a good father*, she thought as she slipped the car into gear. *And he's been through a lot. But I still think I'm going to stay out of his way.*

Chapter Five

The apartment hunting did not go well that day. Heather looked at three tiny places with rents so high she couldn't believe her ears when the real estate lady told her. *So much for those end-of-the-summer bargains Jess had talked about*, she thought to herself. But the sky-high rent wasn't the only problem. From the condition of the apartments, Heather was certain all three had been used by Keats's summer workers as a kind of dormitory. She knew because she'd done the same thing herself, not here in Keats but in nearby Aspen, where she had waited tables one summer. That was between her freshman and sophomore years in college. The pay wasn't good but the tips weren't bad, and she managed to save enough for a full semester's tuition by sharing a small place with four friends. She knew that was what she was looking at here. All three places needed painting badly as well as a thorough carpet cleaning. And they were so small.

She headed back to Denver, discouraged at the prospects for her living conditions in spite of Jess's assurance that "everything will work out." She handled the business of her resignation as simply and directly as possible and was glad when that unpleasantness was out of the way. She packed most of her clothes and returned to Keats the following Monday. She had only one week before the start of teacher workdays, five days in her new school building for meetings and preparation time, and she was determined to find an apartment by then.

But it wasn't to be. Few apartments were going on the market, and one that she really liked was snapped up while she was trying to make up her mind. She would have to be more decisive. So, by the end of the week, Heather was still firmly planted with Jess and Jerry, and she was already convinced she was disrupting their family. She had almost decided she would make the daily drive back and forth from Denver rather than be a burden to them. When she introduced herself at the first meeting at Keats Elementary on Monday morning, she alluded to the problem she was having finding a place to live. And a roomful of nodding heads let her know the problem was a common one.

She liked the staff at first sight. Many of the teachers were young, but she noticed a sprinkling of age to provide a good balance. She was one of only three newcomers, but everyone was friendly. At the coffee break following the first meeting, she had her first chance to put names with faces. Those she spoke with welcomed her warmly and assured her of their willingness to help. She wasn't so certain about the principal, Miss Nordway, though. She talked of the Keats staff being one big, happy family, but unless Heather missed her guess, the woman had an unsettling way of making individuals feel uncomfortable, like when she hoped a certain teacher, Mrs. Burns, Heather thought it was, had gotten plenty of rest during the summer. She must have meant something by it, because the teacher in the spotlight blushed crimson. And the laughter was purely token. Could it be they were waiting for their turn? Heather wondered as she watched the pinched-faced woman, impeccably dressed in a perfectly tailored blue suit, sweep the group of teachers with decidedly cold eyes. *Time will tell*, Heather decided.

She had a chance to look over her room right after the morning meeting. The afternoon session was to include presentations by the nurse, the music teacher, and the art coordinator. For the rest of the week, half of each day, alternating between morning and afternoon, would be given over to such meetings, with the rest of the time for planning and room preparation.

Heather was pleased with her classroom at first glance. She had plenty of chalkboard space, and one wall was totally tackable. She could bulletin-board to her heart's content. This was one of three fourth-grade classrooms. Mary Lane was right across the hall. Heather already felt a camaraderie with her after the hiring interview. A Mr. Jonas Slama occupied the other fourth-grade slot just one door down from Heather. He was one of three males on the staff, and she had not yet met him.

Heather's exploring uncovered a hidden treasure of maps, overheads, prints, tests, and the like in a closet. She busied herself going through what she had found to see what could be used and what should be pitched. She was down on her knees digging in the back of the closet.

"Excuse me."

Heather spun around. One of the teachers she had met earlier was standing in the doorway. She put her memory skills to work. "Oh, hi. It's Shirley, isn't it?"

"Very good." The other woman smiled appreciatively.

"Shirley Merrill. Right?"

"I *am* impressed. How do you do that? I'm still calling people 'hey there' for six months after I meet them."

"Oh, it's just a little memory trick," Heather said as she stood up. She didn't add that she remembered this woman especially because she was the tallest person at the meeting, even counting the three men on the faculty. She studied her from across the room. She was slender with brown hair bleached by the sun and cut short. And she had the deepest blue eyes. Actually Heather couldn't see her eyes from where she stood, but she remembered them from the meeting. They were that distinctive.

"Well, you have to teach me that trick sometime. It's terrible when you teach first grade, and you can't tell one little kid from another. By the time I learn their names, they're moving on to second grade. So I figure, Why bother? Some of the little tykes barely know their own names anyway."

Heather laughed out loud. "Please tell me you're exaggerating."

Shirley grinned. "Well, maybe just a little." She took another step into the room. "I won't keep you from your work, but a bunch of us are going to lunch, and we wondered if you'd like to come along. We try to take advantage of this last week. Next week we'll be on lunchroom duty."

Heather smiled. "Don't I know it." She flicked a wisp of hair out of her eyes. "Sure, I'd love to go. I brought a sandwich, but it will keep. Sounds like a good chance to meet a few people."

"Great. It's settled then. We'll meet by the main office at eleven-thirty." She turned for the door. "If you get finished there, I've got a closet you can start on."

Heather grimaced. "No, thanks. But I will say I'm finding lots of good stuff in here. Who does it belong to, anyway?"

"Ellen Richardson. But don't worry. She won't be needing it where she went. She married a commercial fisherman in Alaska this summer. We're still trying to figure out how that all came about. Nobody around here ever saw the man, but she just up and left right after school was out. Could have been one of those Internet romances, for all I know. A friend of hers told me just this morning that she left all kinds of stuff in her apartment too. He must have been some kind of catch." A sudden smile crossed Shirley's face. "A catch. Get it? Fisherman—catch. Sometimes I totally amaze myself."

Heather chuckled. She was beginning to like this woman, puns and all.

"Sooo," Shirley continued, "dig around in there as much as you like. Nobody's going to stop you. Well, I'd better get back at it. I'm in the middle of bulletin boards. I've never seen a school with so much tack space. See ya."

Heather smiled as she watched Shirley slip out the door. Apparently not everyone enjoyed doing bulletin boards as much as she did.

Shirley wasn't kidding when she mentioned a bunch. There were ten women in all, counting Heather, and they took two cars downtown to Emilio's on the top floor of the Forum, a collection of shops created when the old Essen House Hotel was refurbished some years earlier. Emilio himself greeted them, and they opted for lunch outside in the courtyard, the day being another perfect one, with a blue sky, mild temperature, and no sign of the mountain clouds that usually stirred up a shower or two in the afternoon. From her side of the table, Heather could see Keats's most famous architectural feature, the red brick town hall with its four-story clock tower. The building had been renovated not more than two years earlier and now housed a museum tracing the mining past of the area. She also had a perfect view of Big Bear Mountain in all its splendor.

When they were settled, Shirley insisted Heather show off her memory skills by naming each teacher seated around the table. Heather could tell by the smirk on Shirley's face that she expected failure, but Heather surprised her with a perfect score, including last names.

"How do you *do* that?" Shirley said, shaking her head. This time she was more than surprised; she was mystified by such a talent. Heather smiled knowingly back at her.

Lunch was a great ice-breaker for Heather. The others made her feel at home. She was convinced that if she were dropped in the middle of about any group of elementary teachers anywhere in the United States, she would hear the same talk. She heard warnings about certain parents, concern over standardized tests, and whispered talk about who would have the honor of dealing with the school's rogues' gallery this year, assuming something miraculous hadn't transpired during the summer to turn those troublemakers into model citizens. Heather learned that class lists would be distributed on Friday. She also had her suspicions confirmed about the principal. She was sitting next to Gloria Burns, the teacher in the hot seat during the morning session. She was still more than a little upset over Miss Nordway's remark about getting enough sleep during the summer.

She confided the story to Heather, but the others listened in. "I was late one time last year because my babysitter had a car accident coming to my house. Miss Nordway had to take over my class for maybe twenty minutes. Definitely not more than thirty. I didn't think she believed me when I told her what happened, and now I know she didn't after what she said today. What really gets me is that's the only time I was late all year. All year long! I even made it on time when we had that really bad snow. Usually I'm there at least forty minutes before the kids, more like an hour. Isn't that right, Darla?" She turned to the woman sitting next to her.

"Definitely. You're always in your room working when I walk by."

"I think you should say something to her. Don't let her get away with it," said Ingrid from the head of the table.

"I thought that too," Gloria responded, "but it seems so long ago."

"But she's the one who's still talking about it," Shirley added. "You know how she is. She gets something in her head and won't let go of it. Remember how she was when one of Ellen's kids reworked the letters on her bulletin board into something X-rated? She was talking about that for two years at faculty meetings. She always made it sound like it was Ellen's fault.''

"Maybe you're right," said Gloria thoughtfully, "but it seems so petty. What am I going to do, anyway? Bring in the accident report?''

Heather left lunch happy she had made some new friends, but definitely wary of her new principal.

The afternoon meetings were especially helpful to Heather, new to the system, but she wondered how many times the veterans had been through the same thing. A glance at their glazed eyes provided her with a pretty good answer to that question. As she filed out of the library, she felt a tap on her shoulder. She turned to see Shirley a couple of places behind her. "Wait up," the other woman said. Heather stopped just outside the door so Shirley could catch up. "Come to my room for a second. I want to ask you something.''

Heather rushed to keep up with Shirley's long stride, wondering what was on her mind. She followed her into a bright, colorful room, and her eyes went immediately to a beautiful display that used literally all of one wall of the room. It included mountains and trees and a lake and birds and deer and a path meandering through it that led to a real path coming off the wall and ending in front of a playhouse.

"That is beautiful," Heather said. "I thought you said you didn't like to do bulletin boards?''

"No, I didn't exactly say that. I just said I'd never seen a school with so much tack space. I figure if it's there I might as well use it.''

"You don't put up a new one every year, do you?''

"Well, actually I do. I'm starting my eighth year, and I've had a new one every year. Kids I've had before always stop in to see what's new. They even come back from middle school.''

"How long did this take you?''

"Um, longer than I care to admit. I started the first week in August, and I've been at it, off and on, since then.''

Heather stood admiring the creation. "Well, that is really

something. It makes what I was planning look pretty piddling by comparison.''

Shirley leaned against the top of her desk. ''Please, you're embarrassing me. Anyway, I didn't ask you in here to go crazy over my tack space. I've been thinking about something all day since you mentioned your problems about finding a place to live. I've got a condo over on Rayburn Road. I had a roommate for the past four years, but she moved to L.A. this summer to join some big law firm. I'd pretty much decided I could swing the rent myself, but it seems kind of stupid when I've got loads of room and you need a place. How about it?''

Now Heather knew what had been going on earlier—the visit to her room and then lunch. Shirley had been sizing her up. She must have passed muster, anyway. She should have been doing her own evaluating. Shirley seemed nice enough, but what did she really know about her? And she didn't know if she was ready for the roommate thing again. That took her way back to college days. Still, the apartment possibilities were looking pretty bleak. ''I don't know. I hadn't really thought about the roommate bit.''

Shirley was reading her mind. ''I know what you mean. But I guarantee you I'm not an ax murderer or anything. You aren't either, are you?'' she asked with a sudden grin.

Heather laughed. ''No, I've never been accused of any murders.''

''I'll tell you what. If you have the time, follow me home and look the place over. Then think about it for a couple days, if you like. Okay?''

''Sure,'' Heather answered. ''Why not.''

As Heather followed Shirley on Highway 17 on the way out of town, she was beginning to think that maybe the idea wasn't half bad. They passed the golf course on the left, with its expanse of neatly trimmed contoured grass and sand bunkers and carpet greens. She'd played there a time or two and remembered how difficult the course was. She had lost every ball she had in her bag the first time she played and had to borrow some from her dad to finish the round.

On the right was the cabin of Joshua Keats, the town's founder, and halfway up a low mountain behind his homestead she could see the white tailings from his early silver mine. The crowded parking lot suggested that the mine tour was still popular for summer travelers. She'd been to the mine herself years before with her folks, and she knew the story of Joshua Keats, who had dug a fortune out of that very hole in the side of the mountain in the 1870s and then lost most of it when the mines gave out in the 1890s and the price of silver hit bottom. Joshua spent the rest of his days running a general store in the town that had already been named for him in honor of his early exploits. He died in the late 1920s, just before the automobile gave Keats its second boom, this time in the tourist trade. But it wasn't until the late 1950s that the ski craze turned Keats into a year-round bonanza.

Shirley up ahead slowed and turned into a complex of cedar and glass low-lying condos seemingly growing out of the base of a mountain—Mt. Lander, Heather thought it was. She obviously had driven by these condos a number of times on her way to Bear Claw Ski Resort, which was only about two miles farther ahead, but for the life of her, she couldn't remember having seen them, they were so suited to their setting. *Founder's Place*, she read on a carved wooden sign. *That's fitting,* she thought.

She fell in love with Shirley's place at first sight. The living room was all high ceiling and glass, with a stone fireplace and cedar trim thrown in for good measure. The bedroom that would be hers was spacious and open, with a huge walk-in closet. Shirley pointed out that her former roommate's leaving had also left a huge dent in the furnishing of the place, and Heather could see that her things would fill the void nicely. They sat on the deck and sipped an iced tea, and that clinched it. Not that the view was breathtaking, but it was still beautiful and so much a part of the mountains. The tallest mountains were shielded from view mainly because the complex was so close to them. Who could complain about that? Heather thought. She knew you could expect to pay a forty-thousand-dollar premium for the privilege of seeing snowcapped Big Bear from your living-room window. But how much better to be living right in the middle of the mountains. *It's like camping without all the inconveniences*, she decided.

So it was a done deal. She learned that Shirley was from Milwaukee and was a graduate of the University of Wisconsin.

Like Heather, she had first visited Keats with her folks when she was just a kid and had dreamed of coming here to live ever since. She had just turned thirty less than a week ago, and she still hadn't adjusted to the new decade. She admitted being more than a little nuts about hiking and skiing, and Heather smiled to herself about having guessed that much already. And she was dating the ski director at Bear Claw. *Hello, free ski-lift tickets*, Heather thought with relish.

Chapter Six

The first hint of clouds forming in Heather's new life came on Friday afternoon with the distribution of class lists. The printed lists were placed in teacher mailboxes in the office to be picked up by them as they left for the day. Heather heard groans from those around her as they stood by their mailboxes scanning the lists, and the sounds grated on her ears. She had never liked the idea of preconceived notions about students, notions that were, after all, nothing more than the opinions of someone else. At least she would be free of that this year except for the ominous cumulative folders, which she vowed only to use if necessary.

Since she had little or no knowledge of the history of any of the students in the school, she didn't expect the list to have much concern for her. And she definitely preferred it that way. But she scanned her list anyway. She saw names starting with H and I and a couple of Js all the way to O, the middle of the alphabet, but something out of place caught her eye. She started at the beginning more slowly. The first name started with an A, and the next jumped to an H. She looked more closely. *Adams, Jason*, she read. "Oh, no," she said aloud before she could stop herself. Teachers on either side examining their lists smiled knowingly, and Heather reddened when she realized she was guilty of the same behavior she had been critical of in them only a few moments ago.

She stuffed the list in her briefcase and headed for the door. She was moving over the weekend—the hard way, with a rented truck and old friends from Denver—and she didn't need something like this to weigh on her mind. But it did weigh heavily all the way back to Denver—down Interstate 70, over Loveland

Pass, and through the Eisenhower Tunnel. It was the obvious placement of Marc Adams's son in her class that really troubled her. If it had happened by the luck of the computer shuffle, that would be one thing, she thought, but this way . . . *Suppose another teacher requested he be moved out of her room? Or does this have something to do with Miss Nordway. I wouldn't be surprised.*

And then she allowed herself to think about the real problem. It wasn't about Jason Adams. Sure, Jess had mentioned he was having trouble in school, but she hadn't met a nine-year-old she didn't think she could handle. It was his father she was worried about. She replayed her confrontation with him all over again. *He is so arrogant and so opinionated and so . . . so wrong,* she thought to herself. *I don't know how I'm going to deal with that man. He's just impossible. Now, Heather,* she consoled herself, *you don't have the father in class; you have the son. What's the worst he can do to you? He probably can't get you fired because he couldn't keep them from hiring you.* But she had had enough experience with some parents to know they could be a thorn in the side even when they weren't trying. She wondered how bad it could be if one *was* trying.

With herculean willpower she forced into a corner of her mind her thoughts about what awaited her Monday morning and in the days and weeks ahead. And she was reasonably successful with the effort, mainly because she was working so hard she barely had time to think about anything. It was good to see her friends again. They all pitched in, and by the end of the day Saturday she was properly settled in her shared condo, and Shirley had become fast friends with the crowd from Denver, already arranging for a ski weekend as soon as the first powder fell.

Then there was just Sunday to deal with, a nerve-racking day before the first day of school that had dealt her fits since her first year of teaching. She used the afternoon to make final preparations and then slept fitfully that night, dreaming horrible dreams all night about a classroom where everything that could possibly go wrong, did go wrong.

Chapter Seven

Heather was sitting on the edge of her desk, flashing her brightest smile for the boys and girls as they filed into the room in twos and threes, noisy outside the door but suddenly quiet as they caught sight of the new teacher. She could see them eyeing her coldly, assessing her, arriving at their conclusions. They knew nothing about her, and she knew nothing about them, or next to nothing.

She had dressed her best for this tough audience. She was wearing a light gray pleated skirt and a bright red cotton sweater. The weather in Keats was cool enough in late August to warrant an early fall look. She had arrived extra early this first day. Now that she knew the size of her class, twenty-six, she needed time to arrange the room into five work areas with five desks in each and an extra desk in one. She had placed a packet on each desk with each student's name boldly printed across the top as a way of organizing the seating.

The girls and boys milled around quietly, searching the desks for their names. A few, who hadn't noticed the names on the packets, had to be nudged out of their places by the correct occupants, and wandered frantically until their eyes fell with obvious relief on their own name. Heather had compared her class roster with the names on the packets at least four times to be absolutely certain no boy or girl would suffer the embarrassment of not having an assigned desk. She even had five of the packets prepared and ready on her desk for any late additions to the class.

The packet she had prepared for each student had a letter addressed to parents or guardians introducing herself and explaining her objectives for the year, including what to expect in the way of homework. Another letter, actually the one that doubled as each student's seating assignment, outlined her expectations and grading procedure. And she had included a reading list and a list of possible class field trips.

The room began to fill. As the boys and girls settled in their places, they first looked over the packet in front of them. The noise began to grow as they became more at home and started to chat with those they knew sitting anywhere around them. Some resumed their scrutiny of this Miss DeLaney, especially after they examined her expectations and grading policy. She could see their grimaces and shared unhappiness at the prospect that they would have to work in here. She laughed to herself. It was the same every year. These sunburned, knee-skinned, summer-spoiled boys and girls would have to be tamed all over again—brought back from the world of endless television, sleeping in, and just plain doing nothing to a sense of purpose. And they would kick and scream every inch of the way. But Heather loved it, getting a classroom of nine-year-olds made up of every size and shape and color and attitude to work together.

Then she saw him. His flaming red hair was the only identification she needed, but when she studied his face she recognized him from the brief view she caught of him in the park the other day. It was a different look than she had seen then, though. With his father there had been a look of comfort, of assurance, even of exuberance. There was no exuberance in his face this morning. He entered slowly with downcast eyes, looking neither right nor left. He spoke to no one and sat quickly in an empty seat, one of several Heather had set aside with no name packet in case of any late additions to her roster. He laid his head on the desk—not because he was tired, Heather guessed, but as his ploy to avoid talking with his fellow classmates. It was obvious that Jason Adams did not want to be here. Heather wondered how much his father was to blame for that.

Heather stood and moved toward the boy. The room quieted as she slipped among them. Her movements, her attitudes were still unknown quantities to this crowd. They watched her as she approached the boy with his head down. She stopped by his desk and squatted quickly so her face was even with his. "Good morning," she said. "My name is Miss DeLaney. What's yours?"

The boy jerked his head off the desktop and stared into her face, so close. He thought her smile was pretty, and she didn't have those ugly lines in her face like old Miss Eggers. And she smelled lots better too. ''Jason Adams,'' he said so quietly she could barely hear him. She noticed that their eyes met for only a split second before he looked away.

''Well, Jason Adams, I'm very glad to meet you. I've got a special place for you that I think you'll like lots better than way back here. I'll show you if you'll follow me.''

He got up obediently without a word and walked slowly to the place she pointed out. He buried his face in the letter addressed to him on the desk, but he raised his gaze ever so slightly to study her out of the corner of his eye as she helped another latecomer find his place.

It was well after five o'clock. Heather had finally finished her paperwork to officially open the first day of school. There were census cards, insurance forms, locker registrations, book-condition reports. She had even managed to squeeze in some planning for the next day. Her hope was to establish a normal routine as soon as possible. Like by the second day of school, if she could. She leaned back in her chair and heaved a deep sigh. She was exhausted. She scanned the room, making a mental note of things left to do. She wasn't completely satisfied with her bulletin board on NASA's plans for a probe of the Milky Way's own suspected black hole. She knew she had some good graphics that she had clipped from a news magazine just this summer, but they had been misplaced in the blur of moving. Also she had to review the procedure for accessing the Internet in this building, but that would have to wait until tomorrow. She stood and tucked a few papers in her briefcase and headed for the door.

She walked down the long terrazzo corridor, the sharp click of her steps echoing off the walls. She headed toward the front door but stopped suddenly with a last-minute decision to check her office mailbox. The door to the main office was still unlocked, and she saw lights on in Miss Nordway's office even though there was ample daylight streaming in through the office windows. Without really looking Heather assumed the door to the princi-pal's office was open a crack, because she could hear voices distinctly, one a low-pitched voice, rapid and excited, and the other the slow-paced, controlled tone of Miss Nordway. She couldn't hear what was being said, but she could definitely distinguish the two voices. As she slid open the drawer of her mailbox and began sorting through the stack of papers, mostly new forms for the next day, one of the voices became suddenly loud and demanding. Heather froze in her tracks. Now she recognized that voice. It was Marc Adams, and she could hear his words clearly.

"I want him out of her class!"

Heather felt a tightening in her throat and a weakening in her stomach. She could hear only the murmur of Miss Nordway's response, her voice sounding calm and restrained. Whatever she said didn't seem to satisfy the father of her new student.

"I won't have anyone experimenting with my boy," she heard him say before the door to the principal's office, which Heather now suspected was open more than a crack, was slammed shut. Miss Nordway must have made the same discovery, or maybe she just hadn't expected this parent conference would erupt into such a loud confrontation. The dialogue continued behind the closed door, but Heather could no longer distinguish the words, only voices. It was just as well. She was already agitated beyond measure.

She pushed the mailbox drawer shut and stood for a moment, deciding what to do. She thought seriously about barging into the principal's office to defend herself. After all, she was the one being hashed over in there. But she thought better of that action. She remembered there were channels for such things. And after all, Miss Nordway seemed to have matters under control. In fact, Heather felt a certain admiration for the way the principal was able to stand up to such an irate parent. *But don't get too carried away,* she said to herself. *She may be selling out in there, for all I know. Time will tell. At least I know Jason is prompt about carrying home parent notes.*

She concluded there was nothing to do but leave her fate in the hands of her new principal. She slipped out the office door and hurried from the building, her mind in a spin. It was, she decided, a horrifying experience to overhear someone talking about you in such disparaging terms. Especially for no earthly reason that she could imagine. She certainly was innocent of any sinister manipulation of young minds. What could possibly make him think such things? she wondered.

As she pulled out of the parking lot, she saw a lone car parked in one of the visitors' stalls. As she passed, she couldn't miss seeing the red-haired boy waiting for his father in the front seat of the sedan. *That little boy is the one I feel sorry for,* Heather said to herself. *He needs our help, not all this bickering.*

Try as she might, Heather couldn't get Jason Adams and his father out of her mind all night. If Miss Nordway gave in to an irate parent, that would probably be that. Heather would find a vacant seat in her classroom tomorrow and a change slip informing her of the removal of one of her students. Maybe that would be best all around, she thought. No more confrontations, no second-guessing about everything she attempted in the class. *Then why do you hope that doesn't happen?* she asked herself.

So the second day of school had more than the normal interest for her. She watched as the classroom slowly filled. She surprised her new students with her memory skills as they wandered in by greeting each by name. Jason's place remained empty, a silent reminder of what she had overheard yesterday afternoon. Heather checked the clock. It showed less than a minute before the tardy bell would sound. She moved to close the door, but before she could reach it, the red-haired boy trudged in, head down, on his way to his seat. Heather's face softened into a delighted smile when she spotted him. "Why, good morning, Jason," she said. "I was just beginning to worry about you."

He looked up at her suddenly, surprised to hear his name spoken, and grinned. For only a moment, she saw his freckled face come alive and his eyes shine the way little nine-year-old boys' eyes are supposed to shine. "Good morning, Miss DeLaney," he said, and she had no trouble hearing him. At that moment Heather thought she just might have sacrificed her first paycheck for that grin. So she didn't give in, Heather thought to herself. Now the fun begins.

Chapter Eight

"No, really, I don't want to be in the way. There's nothing worse than a third party along on a date."

"That's silly," Shirley insisted. "I want you to meet Erik. Besides, no one should stay home on a Friday night after the first week of school. It's practically un-American."

"But really, I've got a million things to do. I've got some new worksheets to write and . . ."

Shirley interrupted and clapped her hands over her ears. "No, no, I'm not listening. You're going out tonight, and that's all there is to it."

Erik Sorenson was everything the perfect ski instructor should be. He was tall and lean, with a chiseled face and blue eyes that were almost a match for Shirley's. And of course—Heather smiled to herself—he had to have blond hair that he had pulled into a small ponytail. Heather guessed his delightful Scandinavian accent didn't do him any harm on the slopes either. *You'd better hang on to this one, Shirley,* she thought. *Every ski bunny in Colorado is going to be after him.* But Shirley was a match for him. *In fact,* Heather thought as she looked across at them, *they make a perfect couple.*

The three were enjoying a glass of wine at Timber Lodge, a rough-beamed, rustic place with slowly oscillating ceiling fans and an impressive two-story window with the best view of Big Bear Peak you could get anywhere around Keats. And the food was great.

"You ski, do you?" Erik asked, studying Heather over his glass.

"I try," Heather responded carefully. It was, she thought, like having a race car driver ask if you knew how to drive.

"Don't let her kid you," Shirley broke in. "She's good. She's been skiing since she was this high." She held her hand up to the level of the table.

"Now that is a lie and you know it. I started skiing when I was in high school, but I never get a chance to do it as often as I'd like."

"That will change this winter," Erik said with a grin. He was enjoying the conflict between the two women. "Now you are one of us. Everybody here skis. It is a way of life."

"Well, maybe so, but not everyone skis as well as you."

"Aren't you glad you came along?" Shirley asked. She turned to Erik. "She was going to do schoolwork on a Friday night. I told her that was un-American. Why, I bet that might even be un-European. Don't you think?"

"I don't know. Teachers in my country work very hard because students work very hard. They work much harder than your lazy students," he said with a mischievous grin.

"Now wait just a darn minute, fella," Shirley said, rising to the bait, but she had a grin on her face too. "I won't have you maligning our fine young people. Why, I'll bet your students are just as lazy as ours."

"So this is what I gave up my quiet Friday night for," Heather said, joining in on the fun, "to listen to two people argue about who has the laziest students?"

Heather sat back in her chair. "I can't eat another bite. I don't think I've ever had such a good steak." She cast a quick glance at Shirley. "Too bad we don't have a nice, friendly dog to take these bones home to."

Shirley swallowed her last bite of steak in a gulp. "Don't get any ideas. I don't need a yapping dog to keep me awake at night."

"If you get the right kind, they're as quiet as can be. And they're always so happy to see you when you come home."

"So, Heather, you had a dog back in Denver?" Erik asked.

"Well, no, not really," Heather responded sheepishly. "I wanted one. Dogs weren't allowed in my apartment complex, though. But I had a doggy when I was growing up, a beautiful collie named Stuff.''

''That's a weird name for a dog,'' Shirley said with a grin as she pushed her plate away.

''Well, actually, her name was Stephanie. My mom named her. Of course, they called her Steph, and since I was only like five years old at the time, I got Stuff out of that. So before long she became Stuff to the whole family.''

The waitress had cleared Heather's place and poured coffee. Now that darkness had settled over the mountains, her eyes weren't magnetically attracted to the huge floor-to-ceiling window with its view of Big Bear. She settled back in her chair and took a sip of coffee. The dancing fire in the stone fireplace gave a warm, cozy feeling to the restaurant. Though the room was crowded, the cavernous ceiling seemed to swallow up the talk and laughter going on around them. The mood was almost peaceful.

Heather's gaze rested on a large painting over the fireplace. She hadn't seen it until now, so enthralled was she with the view through the window. The painting showed Big Bear in early fall, with the bright yellow of turning aspen leaves in the foreground. She stared at it motionless. It was an almost living image of the big mountain, but much more. It captured the mountain's strength, its majesty, but also its peace. *How could an artist uncover so much in one painting?* she wondered. *He must love the mountains to be able to do that.* She decided if you couldn't see the real thing out the big window, then certainly this painting had to be the second-best way of enjoying Big Bear.

''Hello. Earth to Heather.''

Heather jerked her head toward Shirley. ''What? Oh, I'm sorry. I was just admiring that painting over the fireplace. It's so beautiful. I guess I couldn't take my eyes off the mountains outside before, but now I can't stop looking at that painting.''

''Do you know who painted it?'' Shirley asked with a slight smirk.

''No, who? I can't read the name from here.''

''Well, I'll give you a big hint.'' Shirley was toying with her new roommate. ''The artist doesn't admire your work nearly as much as you admire his.''

Heather's jaw dropped. "You're kidding! Marc Adams did that?"

"The very same," Shirley responded.

Heather returned to the painting with new eyes. "He's good. He's really good."

Erik twisted in his chair to see what the two were talking about. "Um, not bad," he pronounced.

"Not bad?" Heather questioned in an incredulous tone. "It's fabulous. See how it does more than just photographically record the mountain?"

Erik gave the painting another glance and turned back to the table. "I guess, if you say so. I prefer the real thing. That man, the artist, he is a good skier, though. His son too. I see them on the mountain all the time. Another of his paintings hangs in the lodge. Have you seen it?"

"Can't say that I have," Heather answered. "I guess I've never spent much time in the lodge. I never wanted to lose any ski time."

Erik nodded approvingly. "Ah, you are a real skier then."

"You ought to visit his gallery downtown, if you like his stuff so much," Shirley said.

"Oh, right, like I want to run into the guy."

"Well, you're going to have to run into him sometime. Remember we have a little thing around here called parent-teacher conferences. Ever hear of them?"

"Don't remind me," Heather said with a grimace. She gazed back at the painting. "You say he has a gallery downtown? Maybe I can find out from my cousin Jess if he hangs around there."

The next morning Heather had a quick breakfast before she called Jess. They chatted about the week, and Heather accepted a Sunday dinner invitation before she finally got around to what she really wanted to know. And her cousin didn't let her down. She was a good friend of Doris, one of Marc Adams's gallery workers, and Doris had told her that Marc never came to the gallery before noon, and he usually worked in his studio there for two or three hours every afternoon. So Heather could visit in the morning with no fear that she would run into him there.

She was just ready to go out the front door when Shirley came out of her room rubbing the sleep out of her eyes. "Where are you off to?" she asked through a yawn.

"Downtown."

"What for?"

"Oh, I just have an errand to run."

Shirley's memory clicked in. "Oh, I know. You're going to the gallery. That painting must have made some impression."

"Oh, I'm just curious. Maybe I can learn something about the father that will help with the son."

"Yeah, sure," Shirley said with a note of skepticism in her voice. "Well, don't be disappointed."

Heather's hand was on the doorknob. "Why? What do you mean? Why should I be disappointed?"

"Oh, just because. They say he isn't doing his best work right now."

Heather shrugged and slipped out the door. *I find it hard to believe that someone who can paint as well as he can wouldn't be doing good work,* she thought as she walked to her car. She started to open the door and stopped suddenly. *You're starting to forget,* she said to herself, and took a deep breath of the pine-scented mountain air before she looked about her at the mountains.

She had to park in a public lot several blocks from the center of the small town even though it was fairly early. But it was Saturday, she knew, and the tourists packed in on the weekends even during the off-season. She walked quickly down Glacier Avenue, Keats's main street, dodging early shoppers eager for a memento to take home. Jess had given her directions to Marc Adams's gallery. It was a block off the main street, one of a series of connected shops with a boardwalk running in front. She walked slowly past a wood-carving shop, one devoted to leatherwork, a rock shop, and a glassblower's establishment, with its splashes of colored glass in the window reflecting the early morning sun.

She saw a sign ahead suspended above the boardwalk that said simply *The Gallery.* Beneath it in smaller letters it read *Marc Adams Studio and Collection.* A similar sign another twenty feet

ahead proclaimed simply *The Co-op.* It occurred to Heather that
these two galleries might once have been a single shop. They
shared the same front, huge slabs of glass encased in metal
frames, leaning in toward the gallery in the manner of giant solar
panels. She guessed their position was intended to catch the max-
imum sun.

The door was open and she stepped tentatively inside. She was
still wary about running into the owner himself. A woman sitting
at an oak desk cluttered with papers and empty coffee cups put
down a paperback and got up quickly.

"Good morning. Beautiful day, isn't it?" she said.

"Yes, perfect," Heather responded. She wondered if the
pleasant-looking woman was Jess's friend Doris, but decided not
to make herself known.

"Do you know Mr. Adams's work?" the other woman asked.

"Not really," Heather said.

The woman handed her a small sheet of paper. "This will tell
you something about him. Feel free to look around. Would you
like a cup of coffee?"

"No, thank you. I'm fine." The woman nodded and walked
slowly back to the desk. Heather moved toward a far wall, reading the sheet about Marc Adams as she walked.

Marc J. Adams
University of Colorado—B.A., 1986
University of Chicago—M.F.A, 1988
Postgraduate work—École des Beaux Arts, Paris, 1989
Awards—Paxton Foundation Prize, Midwestern Artist As-
        sociation Fellow, Stuhr Landscape Prize, Eilers
        Award, Fred W. Renslow Merit Award
Permanent Collections—Metropolitan Museum of Art, New
        York City

Heather's eyebrows rose. There was more on the bio, much
more, but she would read it later. She was already mightily impressed. *The Metropolitan,* she thought in shock. *This guy must
be good.* With even greater interest she focused on the first painting in front of her. It was a swirl of gray on a dark background
with a splash of white in one lower corner. She hated to say it

but, to her, the white splash looked as if a brush might have been cleaned there. She moved to the next one. It was similar to the first, but without the white splash. She moved deeper into the room under the loft where she assumed Marc Adams kept his studio. The paintings on the back wall, shaded by the loft outcrop from the natural light flooding into the front of the gallery, were illuminated by spots hanging from the ceiling. Heather moved slowly from painting to painting, a heavy feeling growing in her chest. She stole a quick look at the paintings ahead of her on the opposite wall for any sign of color, any hint of what she had seen in the restaurant last night. But all that met her eye was canvas after canvas of dark abstract design.

She finished her circuit of the paintings with one thought on her mind: she wanted desperately to get away from this place. She was more afraid than ever of running into the man. What would she say to him? She was no expert, but something was terribly wrong here. A man with the talent she had seen and the background described on his bio sheet shouldn't be doing work like this. She had to get away. She glided quickly toward the door, but the woman rose to intercept her.

"Any questions?" she asked with a smile.

"No, thank you," Heather mumbled. She was almost to the door. "Very interesting." She fidgeted with the paper in her hand.

"Yes, aren't they?" the woman replied with that smile.

"Well, thanks again," Heather said as she slipped out the door.

"Come back anytime," she heard the woman say as she retraced her steps on the boardwalk. She hurried to her car with her thoughts in confusion. Now she knew what Shirley had meant. She needed to know more about this man, and she knew who could tell her.

She was in Jess's kitchen in fifteen minutes, a mug of coffee in her hand. "No, that wasn't my friend Doris," Jess was saying as she loaded breakfast dishes into the dishwasher. "She doesn't work on the weekend. That would be Becky Spooner. Tall, skinny, long face? Looks like sugar wouldn't melt in her mouth?" Heather nodded. "Yeah, that's Becky. No, you'd like Doris. She'd talk your leg off and then start on an arm."

Heather's smile was a restrained one. "When we talked about Marc Adams that afternoon of the interview, you never really said much about his art."

"He's good. Or, I should say, he was good."

"What do you mean?"

"He hasn't done anything much since his wife and daughter died. Doris told me he didn't finish a new painting for at least nine months after the accident. She knew he was struggling, everybody did, but nobody could do anything. She said he used to sit up in that loft of his all afternoon in front of a blank canvas, just staring. She'd bring him coffee and try to talk, but he wouldn't say a word. He just stared into space. She said it was spooky."

"That's terrible."

"I know, isn't it? Then she said when he finally turned out something it was one of those bleak things, not like what he'd been doing before. And that's all he ever does, one after the other, all pretty much the same." Jess poured a cup of coffee and sat down across from Heather. "What's the deal? How come you're all worked up about the guy after the way he treated you?"

"I didn't tell you this, but I've got his son in my class."

"Hello!" Jess turned her eyes toward the ceiling. "That's got Miss Myway Nordway written all over it."

"What do you mean?"

"Simple. I told you his boy's not been doing well at school. The dad's been causing trouble. Blaming it all on the school. You know how that goes. It's always the school's fault. I'm guessing Miss Nordway found a way to get even. She put his boy in class with the teacher he didn't want to hire. Since he's complaining all the time anyway, she'll give him something to complain about. And he can't go running to the superintendent because he already made a fool of himself on the hiring committee. Seems like perfect payback time for her."

"So she did put him in my class on purpose."

"Sounds like it to me.

"She's that calculating?"

"Let me tell you something about Janis Nordway. She's a tough principal. Runs a good school, but don't ever cross her. She doesn't forget. She'll figure out some way to get back, like she's doing with Marc Adams. This is probably just the start. She's not through with him yet.''

Heather shook her head. ''Then why in the world would they have him, of all people, on a hiring committee?'' she asked.

''I bet that's none of Nordway's doing. I think he's a friend of Dr. Shoemaker. And I bet the good doctor thought if he got him involved, he'd mellow out. You teacher types are all alike. Always trying to save someone.''

Heather smiled. ''Yeah, right. Well, that was one little saving job that sure backfired.'' She took a sip of coffee. ''It really is sad, though. What that man has been going through. You can see it in his paintings. The difference between what he was doing before and what he's doing now is like day and night. Of course, I've seen only one of the early paintings, but it was so good.''

''Oh, you're absolutely right. Those earlier ones are good. He's made quite a name for himself, considering his age. Why, did you see he has paintings hanging in places all over the world? I've seen some around town. But did you notice the prices on those things?'' Heather nodded, rolling her eyes. ''The gallery where I work doesn't even handle anything that expensive. That's museum stuff. You have to be rich to afford that. Jerry and I always wanted one of his early landscapes, but they were way out of our league.''

''Are they still selling? I mean the new ones?''

''Doris says they are, but not like they used to. There are still people who want an original Adams no matter what it looks like. But interest is definitely falling off, according to her.''

Heather sighed. ''What a shame. All that talent and it's like he's forgotten how to use it.''

''You wouldn't be getting any saving ideas of your own, would you?'' Jess asked with a raised eyebrow.

Heather straightened in her chair. ''Who? Me? Of course not. I'm thinking about Jason. He's been growing up in the middle of all that. And he seems like such a sweet little boy.''

Now Jess raised both eyebrows as she stared at her cousin. ''Well, if you get yourself in the saving business, don't get in over your head.''

Chapter Nine

The weeks literally flew by for Heather. She was so busy with school she scarcely had time to enjoy her new surroundings. But this Saturday she had promised to go with Jess on a hike to Thunder Lake. Jess had planned this outing as a break from the kids. Jerry had soccer duty.

The aspens were just beginning to turn, and the aspen groves seemed alive on either side of the trail as they hiked. The tiny yellow leaves rustled with even the slightest breeze. Heather had hiked with Jess before and knew that, even for her small size, she could set a good pace. She had all she could do to keep up with her cousin.

Once at the lake they enjoyed a lunch of sandwiches and chips and watched a family of ducks that had grown up on the lake over the summer. The two laughed as the ducks, one after another, dived in search of food, leaving their feathery bottoms upturned at the surface. Heather followed the ducks along the shore, trying to snap a picture of all eight bottoms in the air at one time, but one family member always seemed unwilling to cooperate. She finally gave up and came back to take half a roll of shots of Jess feeding potato chips to a chipmunk who was a master at begging for his lunch.

She climbed onto a refrigerator-size flat rock, then took off her floppy hiking hat to get some sun on her face, and lay back, closing her eyes. "This is the life." She sighed aloud.

"I've been trying to tell you that," Jess said. She was trying to convince the persistent chipmunk that he had devoured the last potato chip. "Git now. That's all, buddy. No more left. Find somebody else to mooch off of." She found her own rock closer

46

to the lake. "Once you get married and have a family you don't have time to get away like this. You owe it to yourself. Especially where we live. It's been three weeks since school started, and I bet you've hardly looked at the mountains."

Heather protested. "Oh, I've looked at them, all right, but not much more than that."

"That's what I thought. What's the sense of living in such a beautiful place if you don't get out once in a while? The work will be there when you get back."

"I know. I just wanted to get off to a good start. I've got my boards up and things pretty well in shape. I promise I'll start enjoying myself more."

"Things are going okay in school? I haven't talked to you for weeks except for a few minutes on the phone."

"I know. Yes, everything's great. I've got a good bunch."

Jess sat up and waved her hat at the chipmunk, who had followed her to the rock. "Git. Go home. I don't have anything for you." She lay back down and squinted at the sun. "Even the Adams boy? I know you were worried about him. And his father."

Heather sat up and looked over at the other rock. "I haven't heard a word from his father, which is fine with me. But Jason's been doing so well. I don't know if I told you, but he was so quiet when he first came to class. Wouldn't talk to anyone else. He talked so softly I could hardly hear him. He's lots better now. Even raises his hand to answer questions."

"So how did you manage that?"

"I just try to get him involved. I ask him questions. When we do group work, I put him in charge of a group once in a while, and he does a good job. He eats lunch with the kids now. At first, he sat all by himself during lunch. It was just breaking my heart. So I made up a game."

"Like what?" Jess asked as she sat up to flick an ant off her knee.

"Well, we had a drawing to see who would play the part of Benjamin Franklin for a week at lunch. Jason won." She raised a hand. "Don't ask. Yes, I cheated. Don't ever put me in charge of a drawing. I can't be trusted."

Jess laughed and fell back onto the rock. "I'll remember that. So what then?"

"I gave the new Ben a bunch of handouts about the real Ben, things that would be on a test. The kids were supposed to invite Ben to lunch, a different row each day, and pump him about his life."

"And?"

"And Jason practically became Benjamin Franklin. He learned more about Ben Franklin than I ever had on my handouts. He even brought a kite one day with a big key on it. Scared me to death. I spent the afternoon warning them about how dangerous it was to fly a kite in a storm. So the kids were fighting over whose turn it was to have lunch with Ben Franklin."

"Clever. You must take after our side of the family. So it carried over to when he became just regular Jason Adams?"

"Pretty much. He seems to be a part of a regular group. In fact, just the other day I had to tell him to stop talking during silent reading time. *That* was a first."

Jess sat up again and brushed at her leg. "How come nothing's bothering you? I've got chipmunks crawling all over me, and ants, and a deerfly just took a chunk out of my leg." She stood up. "And not a word from dear old dad through all this?"

"No, nothing. I've just got my fingers crossed that something won't stir him up."

Chapter Ten

It was Monday afternoon. The kids had been gone for about forty-five minutes, and Heather was working at her desk correcting a spelling test she had given that day.

"Excuse me, Miss DeLaney."

Heather looked up. Miss Nordway was standing in the doorway. "Oh, hello, Miss Nordway. Come in."

The principal stepped inside and walked halfway to the desk. She took the opportunity to cast a professional eye about the room—bulletin boards, writing on the chalkboard, maps, displays, orderliness. She liked what she saw. She prided herself on being able to tell if a teacher was getting the job done by looking at her room. She was just ready to compliment Miss DeLaney on her work but stopped the words at the last minute. It was too early to lavish praise on a new teacher. She might quit trying to improve. Besides, there was this business of the phone call. Who knew where that might go?

"Sorry to bother you." She smiled her automatic smile. "I just got a call from one of your parents. He's requesting a conference."

Heather felt a slight chill run up her spine. Parent conferences weren't her favorite cup of tea. "Who?" she asked.

"Jason Adams's father." Heather groaned inwardly but struggled to maintain her composure. "I think we both remember him from your hiring interview," Miss Nordway said. She smiled again.

"Oh, yes," Heather said with a sigh and a grimace. *I just bet you're so surprised,* she thought. "Did he mention what he wanted to talk about?"

49

"No, he didn't say. Have you been having trouble with the Adams boy?"

Heather eyed the principal. *Don't you wish,* she thought. Aloud, she said, "No, he's been doing quite well."

Miss Nordway pursed her lips. "That's good. Well, it's probably nothing then. I told him tomorrow about this time in your room. Is that okay?"

"Sure. That's fine." *That gives me twenty-four hours before I face the firing squad,* she thought.

"Very well, then," the principal said as she turned toward the door. She stopped to align an eraser in its chalkboard tray. "Carry on."

Heather spent the next twenty-four hours racking her brain for some reason to account for the conference. *Maybe it's the kite thing,* she thought. Not that the kite was bad in itself. Actually Heather thought it was a creative addition to his role-playing. But maybe Mr. Adams had been badgered into buying the kite and putting it together. Heather knew kids could be a pain about such things. She seemed to remember her own father digging in the garden at eleven o'clock at night looking for earthworms that she had forgotten to mention she needed for science class the next day. He wasn't too happy about that, as she recalled. Not that he would ever schedule a teacher conference over such foolishness.

And even if it was that kite business, why did he wait so long? That happened almost two weeks ago. She tried to recall anything she might have said that Jason could have related at home in some confusing way. She remembered just last year on election day, she had tried to impress on a class how important it was to vote, and an angry mother called complaining that her little girl refused to go to school because her teacher would find out her parents hadn't voted. Heather learned an important lesson from that one. Teachers wielded a pretty frightening power over the minds of their students. Though she had to admit, most days it was pretty easy to overlook that little nugget of teacher lore, especially when she was correcting a test.

Of course, Heather shared all this with Shirley at home. Shirley listened quietly to all the possible explanations before she offered a simple one of her own. ''Maybe he just wants to tell you what a great job you've been doing. Did you ever think of that?''

''Oh, right,'' Heather said sarcastically. ''Like that's going to happen. You've been spending too much time with first graders.''

She had ushered her twenty-six students out the door some thirty minutes ago. She had been sitting at her desk since then reading the same page of tomorrow's social studies lesson three times, by her last count. She had accomplished something anyway. She had dragged to her desk the only other full-size chair from its place in the corner, where it had been acting as a plant stand for an African violet. She placed the chair in several positions, each time sitting behind her desk to face an imaginary parent until she was satisfied she had it in just the right spot. She admitted to herself, with little shame, that she was trying her darnedest to put him at a disadvantage. If she could have elevated her desk and chair about three feet above his chair, she would have done it in a second. She hadn't forgotten the tone of his voice at that interview, let alone his words. She would love to make him feel like a fourth grader sitting repentant at the teacher's desk.

A sharp rap on the frame of the open door brought her head up. He was standing just inside the room. ''I'm a little early, Miss DeLaney. I hope you don't mind.''

She felt her heart race. It was a first. He was speaking to her in a normal tone of voice. ''No, that's fine. Come in.''

He came toward her desk. He was taller than she remembered. He was wearing khaki pants and a rust-colored pullover sweater. His look was intense, and his lips behind the neatly trimmed beard were rigid and straight, but Heather became convinced by the way he carried himself that he might be just a trifle nervous. After weeks of imagining a parent conference with the man, she was glad to see that he could be human after all. She motioned him to the chair. ''Is it getting cold out?''

''Yes, yes, it is,'' he volunteered.

''Snow can't be far away,'' she said lightly as she sat down. ''I've seen the dustings up in the mountains.'' She looked up and caught him staring at her with those brown eyes she remembered so well.

"We'll be up to our elbows in the stuff before we know what's happening," he said matter-of-factly.

There was a moment of awkward silence as the two studied each other. "You wanted to see me?" Heather finally managed.

"That's right," he said, and crossed an ankle over his thigh. "I'm worried about Jason," he began.

"Oh? In what way?"

"I think he may be working too hard."

Heather knew the look on her face must be betraying her shock. This was a new one on her. She couldn't remember a parent complaining because a child was working too hard. "You mean he has too much homework?"

"Yes, exactly, Miss DeLaney. He's always working on some project. Like this Benjamin Franklin business." *Oh, here comes the kite thing,* Heather thought. He leaned forward. "I mean, he was obsessed with Benjamin Franklin. Morning, noon, and night, Benjamin Franklin. I was sick of hearing about Benjamin Franklin."

Heather smiled. She wanted desperately to suggest that this intense man lighten up a little, but all she could manage was, "Did he tell you he won a drawing to become Benjamin Franklin?" she asked.

"He told me. Seems to me that's a lot to expect from one little boy. My gosh, he was doing the work for the whole class. What in the world were the rest of them doing while he was studying half the night?"

Heather could feel the heat slowly creep up her neck. *Stay in control,* she reminded herself. *Let's not let this degenerate into a slugfest like the hiring thing.* "Their job was to interview Jason to learn what they could about the person he was playing. Everyone in class was tested on that information." She toyed with the idea of telling him the hidden agenda in the lesson, but decided it might be too experimental for his tastes.

"And now it's glacier moraines. We had to take a drive Sunday to find glacier moraines."

Heather nodded. "So that explains why he answered so many questions during today's science lesson. But I assure you, Mr. Adams, he's on his own with that one. We're studying moraines and we're going on a field trip, but I haven't given any outside work.''

''Well, he certainly interpreted whatever you said as meaning he needed to do extra work.''

Heather was getting aggravated in spite of herself. If she had ever been in a stranger parent conference, she couldn't remember it. How could he possibly twist the good things that were happening with his boy into something bad? ''Tell me, Mr. Adams, is all of this extra work, as you call it, having a bad effect on Jason? Does he dislike school? Are you having trouble getting him to go to school?'' Mr. Adams picked nervously at a loose thread on the cuff of his pants.

''Well, no.''

''Isn't it true there were some problems along that line last year?''

He looked up suddenly. ''Why would you say that?''

''Miss Eggers indicated that on his cumulative folder.''

''Jason never got along with Miss Eggers.''

Heather had heard that one before. Last year's teacher was always a favorite target. She found herself enjoying Mr. Adams's discomfort just a little too much. *My turn now,* she thought to herself. *You're in my classroom.* She watched him closely. ''All I can tell you, Mr. Adams, is that Jason is doing excellent work. He's responding well in class. He's turned in every assignment on time, and his test scores have been very good.'' She looked over the class record sheet in front of her. ''And according to my records, he hasn't missed a single day of school.'' *What a strange way to get even with someone,* she thought. *Telling him nothing but good things. He thought I would fall on my face, but I fooled him.* He was staring at her with those dark eyes, and suddenly a faint smile crossed his face. It looked good on him, made him seem less intense, more vulnerable, a look he obviously worked hard to guard against. It struck her that this was the first time she had seen him smile, not counting that day of football between father and son that she had witnessed.

Marc Adams studied his son's teacher. He knew he had been a fool at the hiring interview. Afterward he tried to figure out why he had said what he did. There was something about the confident look of the woman that set him off. He knew it made no sense. Most of what he did and said anymore made no sense. Then when he learned that Jason was in her classroom, the very teacher he did his darnedest to blackball, he just knew she would take it out on his boy. But it hadn't happened. Day after day he waited for the telltale signs. He'd gotten so used to them the last two years. The crying, the bad grades, the notes from the teacher. But none of it happened. Jason was a changed boy. All he talked about was Miss DeLaney, and his eyes sparkled when he told what they were doing in school.

So here he was finding out for himself. Why did he have to come here with a chip on his shoulder? With this ridiculous complaint about overworking his boy? Why couldn't he tell her he was sorry? Why couldn't he tell her he had been wrong about her, that she was doing a good job? *I should be thanking her for what she's doing for Jason,* he thought. Then a new idea struck him. He'd never had to worry about her getting even with him through Jason. She hadn't needed to. She'd been waiting for the old man to show up so she could take aim, and she'd done a pretty good job of putting him in his place. He felt like he'd been kept after school himself. The thought of it was positively hilarious.

"Mr. Adams? Mr. Adams? Are you all right?"

Marc Adams blinked his eyes and looked up into the charming face of his son's fourth-grade teacher. "Yes, yes, I'm fine." He got to his feet so fast it startled her.

"Was there anything else?" she asked, but he was already at the door.

"No, no, nothing. Miss DeLaney, I'm afraid I've wasted your time." She was about to assure him of the contrary even though she believed he was right, but he was already out the door. She rolled her eyes at the ceiling. *That was the strangest conference I have ever been a part of,* she thought, but it wasn't over yet. His face appeared again at the door, and he was smiling, actually smiling. "I'm sorry," he said simply. Then he was gone.

Heather sat stunned at her desk. She wasn't certain what he had just apologized for, but she didn't think it was just for wasting her time.

* * *

Marc climbed into the car next to his son, who balanced the video game he'd been playing on one knee and reached for his seat belt. "Did you see Miss DeLaney, Dad?"

Marc started the car and turned to Jason. "Yes, I did."

"You didn't say anything dumb, did you?"

Marc thought for a moment. "I might have."

"Aw, Dad, why'd you have to go and do that for? Now she's gonna think I'm a big geek."

Marc put the car in gear and headed for the exit. "I assure you she's not going to think you're a big geek. Maybe your dad, but not you. She thinks you're quite a guy."

Jason brightened. "Is that what she said?"

"Well, she didn't use those exact words, but that's what she meant."

Jason beamed. "Isn't she pretty, Dad?"

Marc stopped at the exit to check for traffic. He reached across and tousled the boy's mop of red hair. "Yes, she is, Jason. She really is."

Jason watched his dad as they left the school parking lot, and a new thought worked its way into his nine-year-old brain.

Heather gathered her things, turned off the lights in her room, locked the door, and made her way down the hall to Shirley's first-grade room. The two were riding to school together these days. Shirley was on a chair tacking colorful drawings of Big Bird holding the vowels. She turned as Heather came in. "Hi. I'm almost through here. How'd it go? I saw him go by each way." She stepped down from the chair. "He wasn't there very long."

Heather sat in one of the tiny chairs by the playhouse and set her briefcase beside her. Her knees were practically in her face. "Shirley, that was the strangest conference I've ever been a part of."

Shirley began loading sheets of poster board and markers into a cardboard box to take home. "So what happened? Tell me everything."

"It was weird. You know what he was upset about? He thinks Jason is working too hard."

"You're kidding!"

''That's about what I said. Except I really don't believe that's what he thinks.''

Shirley set the box on a chair and rummaged through a desk drawer for her lunch sack and thermos. ''What do you mean?''

''I don't know. I got the feeling that he wanted to check things out for himself, and he needed an excuse. I'm pretty sure even he knew it was lame.''

Shirley opened a closet near the front of the room and took a light jacket off a hanger. ''So what did you say?''

''I told him how great Jason is doing. That cooled him off.''

Shirley pulled on her jacket and switched off the lights. ''Sounds like you had things under control.''

Heather struggled out of the tiny chair and followed her roommate out the door. ''He said he was sorry.''

Shirley balanced the cardboard box in one hand and locked the door. ''You mean about the conference?''

The two women walked together down the hall toward the front door. ''That's just it. I don't know. I guess it was for the conference, but I got the feeling it might have been for what he said at the hiring interview.''

''He apologized for that?''

''Well, not in so many words, but the way he said it I got the feeling he was trying to say something else.'' Heather swung the front door open and held it for Shirley. ''I don't know. It was so confusing.''

''Well, it's over, anyway. Didn't I say you were worrying for nothing?''

''I guess you're right.'' Heather sighed as she glanced at the distant mountains, where the line of snow at the higher elevations was becoming clearly defined. The two walked in silence for a moment. ''He's not really as bad as I thought he was,'' Heather said suddenly.

''That's interesting coming from you after the way he treated you.'' The two reached Shirley's car, and she put her cardboard box on the top as she fumbled for her keys.

''I know, but if you look into his eyes, he seems so haunted.'' She was remembering his dark, brooding look. ''But he doesn't like what he's become. It's like he's trying to get back to the surface from somewhere deep underwater.'' Now she was re-membering his smile.

Shirley looked over the top of the car at her. ''Have you ever thought about writing some good old, sad country music lyrics?'' She turned her face up to the sky and, in an exaggerated country twang, crooned, '' 'I'm drownin' in a sea of tears for you.' Hey, not bad, huh?''

Heather laughed even though she knew she was being made fun of. ''I mean it. He's been through a lot.'' She climbed in the car as Shirley loaded the box into the backseat and then slid behind the wheel.

''I know he has, but what can we do about it?''

''We can help, that's what,'' Heather said firmly.

Shirley cast a quick glance across the car at her roommate and raised an eyebrow.

Chapter Eleven

Heather had only a minute before the dismissal bell would end the school day, and she had an important announcement. She shouldn't have waited until the last minute, because she could see by the faces of the class that she was going to have a hard time making them listen. "Okay, listen carefully," she began. "I have two important announcements. Remember, we visit the Sheephead Moraine day after tomorrow. I must have your signed parent permission slip back tomorrow or you won't be able to go. You'll have to stay here in the library studying." There was a general groan. Good, she thought, at least they're listening. "Now, more than half of you haven't brought back those sheets. So don't forget."

She was racing the red second hand on the big clock. "Next, I need a parent to ride along on Thursday. If your mom or dad would be available and could ride along, I'd appreciate it." The bell rang and the kids strained at their seats, waiting for Miss DeLaney's official dismissal. She held up several sheets. "If you'd like to take one of these home explaining our field trip, please see me right after school. All right, you may go." There was the usual rush for the door. "Slowly now," she said loudly enough to be heard over the excited din.

She walked to the door to see them down the hall, angry with herself because she hadn't left enough time for her announcements. She'd learned long ago that you didn't save important information for the last five minutes of school. But it had been one of those days. Miss Nordway had approached her just today while she was on lunchroom duty with the little bombshell that all teachers were expected to include at least one parent on every

58

field trip. That was news to her, and she wondered if it was possible at this late date. Miss Nordway's raised eyebrow let her know the principal would be most disappointed if her directive weren't followed. She decided she would have to try some parent phone calls that evening to drum up a volunteer.

The crowd in the hall thinned, and she stepped back into her room. She was surprised to see Jason Adams standing patiently by her desk. He had been doing good work, as she told his father, but he was still more than a little distant. In fact, she had been pleasantly surprised to learn from Mr. Adams that Jason had talked about her in such enthusiastic words at home. To her, he seemed excited about learning new things, but he kept his distance. While other students might hang around her desk before school started or after the lunch period, Jason never did.

"Jason, what can I do for you?" she said with as much lightness as she could put into her voice at the end of a long day. "You don't want to miss your bus."

"No, Miss DeLaney, I won't." He was all business. He smiled more readily now, but he was usually a serious little boy. "I need one of those sheets you told us about."

Heather had to struggle to hide her surprise. "Why, of course. They're right here." She peeled off one of the sheets and handed it to him. "Do you think your dad might like to go along?"

Jason folded the sheet neatly but then crammed it into his backpack before he answered in what Heather interpreted as a first-things-first strategy. He looked at her with brown eyes nearly as dark as his father's. "I hope so," he said matter-of-factly in the manner of a nine-year-old. He pulled the backpack over one shoulder and ran for the door. "Good-bye, Miss DeLaney," he shouted as he raced through the doorway.

"Good-bye, Jason," she called after him, a broad smile forming.

Heather followed her class to the yellow bus parked by the curb. The day was clear but chilly, with a sharp wind making it feel even colder. She was glad she'd worn her wool slacks and bulky sweater and her new all-weather coat. She looked up to see Marc Adams by the bus. She was still in total shock that he had actually agreed to go along, and she had convinced herself that at the last minute he would back out. But there he was, plain as day, standing before her. He was dressed in well-worn jeans and hiking boots that looked as if they had seen plenty of action. He had on a maroon turtleneck sweater and a dark blue windbreaker with a string-tie hood. Heather guessed he might need it, because he wasn't wearing a hat. She smiled at how uncomfortable he looked. He was rocking from one foot to the other with his hands in his jacket pocket. He obviously wasn't in the habit of taking twenty-six fourth graders on a field trip. She smiled again when she remembered the look on Miss Nordway's face when she broke the news that she had a parent volunteer for the field trip and it was none other than Marc Adams.

"Good morning, Mr. Adams," she said as she approached him. "Do you know what you've gotten yourself into?"

He smiled easily, reminding Heather again of how handsome he was when his face lost that intense look that seemed to be so much a part of him. "Don't scare me away. I'm still within running distance of my car."

She laughed. "No, it's not that bad if you can stand a little noise. I appreciate your volunteering. I didn't find out till yesterday that school policy recommends at least one parent chaperon, so it was kind of a last-minute thing."

"Jason can be pretty persuasive when he wants to be."

"I imagine. Most kids have their ways."

The last of the fourth graders had trouped aboard the bus. Heather stepped up inside to survey the situation. Her students were already starting to enjoy their day away from the classroom. She could see nothing but happy faces looking back at her, and the volume of talk and laughter was beginning to build. Her glance fell on one empty seat at the very front right, so thoughtfully left for her. The only other empty seats were far in the back. *This will be an interesting ride,* she thought. She was aware that Mr. Adams had climbed in after her and was on the bottom step at the door. "Shall we share this one?" she said over her shoulder to him and then stepped awkwardly into the aisle to let him get to the window seat without really hearing what he said in reply. She did a quick head count, found everything in order, and nodded to the driver.

She sat carefully on her half of the hard vinyl seat as the front door slapped shut. The driver slipped the big bus into gear, and they rumbled away from the curb.

"As I remember, you said you've been to Sheephead Moraine, Mr. Adams?" Heather asked, turning her head to look at him. She was close enough now to get a hint of his aftershave and to see that his neatly trimmed beard wasn't as red as she thought. She could see in the red the dark brown of his hair.

He tugged on his beard with thumb and forefinger. "Yes, I think I did mention Jason and I were there last weekend. I guess I made that out to be more of a chore than it really was. Jason and I go for hikes quite often." Heather only nodded. She decided not to help him out. *Let him sweat a little after the way he treated me,* she thought. "That isn't the first time I've been there, though," he went on. "I painted it once. Maybe five years ago. I didn't approach it as a geological phenomenon or as an Ice Age wonder or anything like that, though. I'm not sure I even knew about all that at the time. But I liked the texture, the contrast between a pile of boulders and small rocks I found and the mass of mountain behind it. I tried to show that, and it turned out pretty well, I guess."

Heather wasn't sure she wanted to get into the painting thing. Not after she'd seen the work in his gallery, the work he was doing now. She had to admit, though, that what he'd just said sounded like what she would expect from the artist who had painted the Timber Lodge painting. She decided to push on. Maybe she would find out for sure what had made the big change in his work. "I saw one of your paintings just a couple of weeks ago up at Timber Lodge." He nodded, but Heather could see his jaw tighten. "It is *beautiful*. Please understand I know very little about painting, but I know one thing for sure. That painting says exactly what I feel when I'm out here." She gestured toward the window. "I can't really put it into words but it's about how small I feel when I'm in the mountains. And about time. Time has no meaning because those mountains heaved out of the ground so long ago it was before time ever existed." She frowned in frustration. "Oh, I don't know; I can't really explain it."

Marc Adams was watching her as she spoke, and his face had lost its strained look. "And like you're there at the very beginning almost as if it only just happened."

"Yes, that's it. As if Big Bear Peak just rose out of the mist." She was staring ahead of her, imagining the painting she had seen weeks ago, oblivious of the noise of happy nine-year-olds around her. "How do you do that with only a brush and paint? How can you make a painting say so much?"

"Miss DeLaney, I only wish I knew."

"What do you mean? You must know. You created all that beauty."

"I think I did once, but that was a long, long time ago. I've forgotten how. It's gone. Like another person entirely did those things. I use the same canvas, the same brush, the same oils. I stare at a blank canvas for hours at a time, but my mind sees nothing to paint. I'm empty. There's nothing inside."

She had her answer to why his paintings had changed so completely. She had read about the same kind of thing happening to other creative people—writers especially. But usually that kind of thing happened in advanced age when the creative well was dry. This man was in the prime of his life. *He should be doing his best work,* she thought. *His loss has absolutely destroyed him inside. There must be something that can bring him back.* "I'm sorry," she said simply. "But you must keep trying."

He turned toward her and smiled, but it wasn't the soft smile she had seen on his face several times now. It was the old hard smile, and his voice was cynical and sarcastic when he spoke. "But of course. The great Marc Adams can't disappoint his many name-dropping fans. But what I do now is garbage, pure garbage."

He spoke with such bitterness that Heather glanced around her to see if the children were listening, but she had little to worry about on that score. Twenty-six young people were making enough noise to drown out almost anything. But he saw her concern. "I'm sorry. Let's talk about something else. It's not safe to mention art in my presence." He turned and stared out the window. The bus was winding its way through a forest of pine down into a valley carved by a wall of ice thousands of years ago. There they would examine the accumulation of rocks and boulders left behind by a giant glacier when it melted slowly over eons.

"Miss DeLaney, Miss DeLaney."

Heather turned at the sound of the shout from the back of the bus. She scanned the rows of young people for the source and saw a hand waving from one of the last seats to attract her attention. "Yes, Adriana, what is it?"

"Gretchen's sick," the little girl called. The noise level dropped as heads turned to see what was happening in the back. "She says she's gonna throw up."

Heather turned back toward Marc and rolled her eyes. "Duty calls," she said as she stood and headed down the aisle. She stayed with the little girl to keep her mind off her motion sickness, and they survived the rest of the trip. The bus pulled to a stop in the parking lot overlooking a wide valley scooped out by the glacier that once sculpted the peaks in its path. Marc hopped out of the bus first and kept the boys and girls together until their teacher climbed down behind Gretchen, who was already feeling much better.

"Everything all right?" he asked when he caught sight of the two of them.

"Yes, she's fine. Just a little motion sickness."

He melted into the background then and watched her do her thing. She led the class down into the valley toward a grouping of boulders that looked as if they had been tossed there carelessly by some giant hand. She described how the scene before them might have looked thousands of years before. She pointed out the dissimilar rocks that had been sliced from the surrounding peaks, churned in the slow-moving mountain of ice, and deposited side by side on the valley floor. She made it all seem more real than he could have imagined. She asked questions. She praised answers. She pointed out rock formations. And she didn't neglect to remind the children of the beauty that was all around them. "Mr. Adams is an artist," he heard her say, much to his surprise. He had assumed he would be nothing more than a silent observer on this field trip. "Maybe he would tell us," she went on, "what the artist's trained eye looks for in a mountain scene like this. Maybe we can get some hints for art class." She turned toward him, and suddenly he was aware of a sea of young faces staring at him expectantly.

He looked toward the uneven silhouette of the mountains in the distance to gather his thoughts, a slight smile playing at his lips at what she had gotten him into. "I guess I look for contrasts," he began slowly. He saw many questioning looks and knew he would have to simplify. "Contrast means difference," he explained. "Like the colors black and white. There's a difference between them, a contrast." He looked back at the mountains. "Sometimes the lighting creates all the contrast you need. Look how the sun is hitting that one peak over there." He pointed toward a distant mountain, and all heads turned in that direction. "See how the light makes a shadow line so you can see all the jaggedness of the rock right at that line? That's contrast. I'd like to paint that. To show the detail just at that point." And as he said it, he became aware that a strange thing was happening inside. He knew that he *did* want to paint it. He felt an urge to capture the brightness of the sun as it splashed on the rock and as it glistened off the snow dusting the dull green firs. He even found himself imagining what oils he would mix to get just the right colors. He could almost feel the smoothness of the brush handle in his hand. He wanted to paint, and he hadn't really wanted to paint for a long time. He studied the mountain then in silence, oblivious of the faces of the children looking from him to Miss DeLaney and back again.

Heather had heard a certain something—a catch of emotion, she decided it was—come into the sound of his voice as he was describing the scene to the children. She could definitely see what he was seeing on that far-off mountain peak. She could even imagine the finished painting, the feeling he would try to capture with it. But the murmur of young voices brought her back suddenly to the valley floor. Startled that she had become so captivated with his explanation, she looked toward him, only to find that he was still studying the mountain.

"Thank you, Mr. Adams," she began, breaking his concentration and bringing him back to the restless pack of young people. "Now we can see how a real artist looks at the mountains. We need to train ourselves to see such detail around us, don't we?" Jason watched his father from where he stood at the edge of the group, a feeling of pride glowing inside him. He had heard something different in his dad's voice, a sound he couldn't remember ever hearing before. He saw the familiar eyes finally look away from the mountains and rest on Miss DeLaney, who was leading the class to one of the boulders in the distance. Jason studied his teacher for a moment, thinking how pretty she was. *So much prettier than old Miss Eggers,* he thought. He glanced quickly back at his dad and his eyes brightened. He hurried to catch up with the others.

"Now, who can tell me what this is growing on the rock?" she was asking as he joined the class.

Jason could barely see over those in front of him, but he knew what she was talking about. He had read about lichens in his computer encyclopedia just last night. He waved his hand in the air. "Yes, Jason?"

"They're lichens," he said, rhyming the strange word with *kitchens.*

"Very good," she said. "But this is one of those unusual words that isn't pronounced the way it's spelled. We've found many of those words in our language, haven't we? Like *knife,* for example. We'll put this word on the board when we get back and you'll see why Jason pronounced it the way he did. It's *liken.* Let's say it together now."

Marc followed along at the fringe of the group as Heather led her students across the valley, stopping to investigate animal tracks along the way and identifying plants as they came to them. He couldn't help noticing the respect the children had for her; it was so plain to see. By some magic she had them wanting to learn, even Jason. No, especially Jason, he decided. Jason had his old zest for school back, a zest that Marc had been so afraid might be lost forever.

On the way back to school, Marc sat in one of the front seats by himself, and Heather shared the other with Gretchen. Marc smiled to himself at Miss DeLaney's constant patter with the little girl to keep her mind off of the possibility of being sick. And it worked. As the students filed into school, Miss DeLaney came to him and extended her hand. "I want to thank you so much for coming along," she said as their eyes met.

He awkwardly shook her hand, which was warm and delicate to the touch, and nervously tugged at his beard. "I don't think I was much help."

"Oh, but you were," she assured him. "I especially liked your artist's view of the mountains. I'd love to see that painting when you finish it.''

"I don't know if that will ever happen," he mumbled.

"I hope it does," she said. "It's such a good idea." She turned to catch up with her students, the last of whom had reached the school door. "Thanks again. 'Bye.''

" 'Bye,'' he responded as he watched her go, convinced that he had learned more that day than any of her students.

Chapter Twelve

Heather maneuvered her car neatly into a tight parking space. It was Saturday, and she was almost late for a hair appointment. She had overslept. Well, that wasn't entirely true. She had been awake in plenty of time, considering it was Saturday morning, but when she glanced out the window by her bed, she saw snow. Not a lot of it—just a thin white blanket sifted evenly over everything. She pulled her quilt up to her chin and smiled lazily at the snug, secure feeling in her cocoon. And, of course, she drifted back to sleep, only to awake with a start thirty minutes later. She had jumped out of bed, thrown on a pair of jeans and a sweatshirt, and grabbed a piece of toast and a glass of juice. And when she had rushed to her car, the snow that she had to brush from her windows didn't seem quite as beautiful as it had earlier. But with this parking space nearly in the heart of downtown Keats, she would make it. Lucky for her the summer tourist season had ended, and the crush of skiers was still weeks away.

She hopped out of the car not more than a half block from her destination—Justine's. Shirley had assured her there wasn't a better salon in town, and she insisted Heather ask for Colette. As she went through the front door, she felt her first real doubts about what she was planning. She had worn her hair long for years now, going back at least to her college days. She usually wore it tied back, often in a French braid, but that took precious time every morning. She was going to try something different, something short. And she wasn't going to have time to talk herself out of it because Colette was ready for her. As she sat in the chair, she wondered how her students would react to the change. She really should have done this before school started, she decided, but it was too late now; Colette was already busy with the scissors.

She avoided the mirror in front of her until Colette announced she was finished. Heather raised her eyes tentatively and stared at the new person in the mirror. She looked so different. Her hair was delicately feathered at the front and sides. The look was casual; she would even say chic. She smiled at herself. She definitely liked what she saw. She left the salon feeling strangely light and bouncy. She passed Brewer's Coffee House and glanced in. There were only one or two tables occupied. She had wanted to try the café latte here on two occasions that she could remember, but the place had been standing room only. Maybe Jess has a point about getting rid of the tourists, she thought to herself as she made a quick turn on the sidewalk and opened the door to such a delicious combination of aromas it made her mouth water in anticipation. She would celebrate her new look.

Brewer's was quiet and peaceful this day, and she picked a cozy table by the front window where she could watch people as they passed. She ordered her latte and settled back in contentment. She took a sip and smiled her approval. As good as any latte she could remember having. She stared dreamily out the window, not really seeing anything, only vaguely noticing the occasional passerby. With a start, she became aware that someone was studying her through the window. Her eyes focused quickly. It was Marc Adams. He smiled and left the window, only to reappear at the front door. She watched as he made his way toward her table. "I didn't mean to stare. I was trying to figure out if it was really you. You look so different."

Heather blushed. *It's beginning already,* she thought. "I decided it was time for a change."

"What a change! Don't get me wrong," he added quickly. "It looks great. Not that there was anything wrong with the way you looked before."

"Why, thank you," Heather said. "I just hope the change won't be too much for my students."

"They'll love it." He was standing with his hands in the pockets of his windbreaker. "Mind if I join you?" he asked.

"Oh, please do."

He sat down and examined her cup. "Café latte?" She nodded. "They make a good one," he said.

"I was just thinking the same thing."

He placed his order and settled back in the chair, studying her. In fact, he couldn't take his eyes off of her. The hair made her look so different. He decided that before, with her hair done up, she looked older, more mature—kind of like you expected a teacher to look, he had to admit. But now she looked athletic, full of life, younger. The new look accented her eyes, for some reason. He had thought when he first saw her how expressive her eyes were. Now they were even more so. He wondered how the kids would take to the new Miss DeLaney. He remembered once when he was ten or eleven and was with his mother, shopping, they had seen the reigning Miss Colorado doing some kind of a promotion in a grocery store, of all places. He had been so stunned by the young woman's beauty that he had been unable to say one single word to her. He had been afraid of her. He wondered if he would be like that now if he were in Miss DeLaney's classroom.

Heather shifted uneasily. "Do I really look that strange?"

"I'm sorry. I was staring again, wasn't I? You really look so different."

She was growing self-conscious about the hair, but she knew she'd better get used to it. She'd have a whole classroom of curious kids staring at her on Monday morning. There was something different about him today too, she decided. He was obviously more relaxed, more at ease, maybe even happier. He had lost that brooding, haunted look in his eyes. The break in his reserve that she had seen a hint of at last week's strange parent conference and then again during the field trip, at least on the bus ride out to the moraine, was now so obvious as not to be missed. She wondered what had happened to cause the change.

"You survived yesterday, I see," he remarked by way of changing the subject.

"Yes, I thought it went very well. By the way, did you notice how well Jason did? He seemed to have all the answers. Is there anything he doesn't know about glaciers?"

Marc smiled broadly at the mention of his boy. His pride was good to see. "Yes, he did all right, didn't he?" He watched her over the brim of his cup as he took a sip of his coffee, and Heather noticed a playful look in his eyes she hadn't seen before. "You mean you aren't going to remind me how important it was to take him on that little drive in the mountains last weekend? You know, when I could have been watching a good football game?"

She gave him a look of her own. "It doesn't hurt fathers to do those little extra things with their sons." As she said it, she remembered the day she had seen father and son playing football together. She guessed such togetherness was not a problem with the two.

They sat in silence for a long moment, but it wasn't the uncomfortable kind, the kind that must be filled. Finally, he spoke. "You really like teaching, don't you?"

"Yes," she said simply. "Why did you say that?"

"Oh, no reason, I guess. I was just thinking that it shows. You're lucky to be doing something you really like to do. What made you become a teacher in the first place?"

Heather thought for a minute. "I guess I never wanted to be anything else. Or at least not that I can remember." She looked back at him, a little embarrassed that she had answered with such intensity. "That sounds really corny, I suppose."

"No, it doesn't," he assured her.

"It sounds like something you'd say at a job interview," she said with a quick smile. Suddenly her face blushed crimson for the second time this morning. She realized too late what she'd said. She definitely hadn't meant to remind him, or herself for that matter, of that horrible interview, especially since things had been going so well between them. But now it sounded like that was exactly what she was trying to do. Trying to extract an apology from him or something. "I didn't mean anything by that," she blurted. "I assure you it was an accident." She met his eyes again with some effort.

He traced a pattern on the glass-topped table with his index finger as he watched her. "I *was* pretty obnoxious that day, wasn't I?"

"Well," she said with a tilt of her head, "now that you mention it . . ."

"I'm sorry. There, I've said it. I've been trying to figure out how to say that for weeks. I know you're not going to believe this, but I think that's what I was trying to tell you when I came to school about Jason, but it didn't come across that way, I know. I sounded like a real pain-in-the-neck parent. As usual,'' he said with emphasis.

He paused for breath, and Heather wondered if she should say something. But for the life of her she couldn't figure out what it would be. There was no denying that what he was saying was true, but shouldn't she help make his apology a little easier? Before she could think of how to do that, he was off again.

''About that first day. The truth is, I walked into that job interview with a chip on my shoulder this big.'' He held his hands apart. ''And I took it out on you. No matter who was there that day, I would have found something wrong. But you didn't back down, and that made me even madder. I thought you were just a little too sure of yourself. It didn't take me too long to find out you had good reason to feel that way.'' He took a deep breath. ''So I hope you can accept my apology. I know it's a little late, but better late than never.''

His almost courtly manner made Heather feel warm inside. ''I've got a little confession of my own,'' she said. ''You made me so angry that day that I put on that little air of confidence just to show you. Apparently it worked a little too well. And by the way,'' she continued with that playful look he was beginning to like, ''I think I owe you for getting me the job.''

''What in the world do you mean?'' he asked in surprise.

''I really think the committee felt sorry for me after you had your say. They practically handed me the job on a silver platter after you left.''

''Good.'' He slapped a fist lightly on the table, but it still made their cups jump. He was amused that his histrionics that day had actually worked in reverse. ''Thank goodness they realized what a jerk I was being and hired you anyway. If they did it to spite me, all the better. But I find that hard to believe. I'm sure you won the job on your own merits. Your credentials were impressive, though I wasn't about to admit it that day.'' He shifted in his chair and crossed his legs. ''But I don't care how it happened, I'm just glad it happened. What you've done for Jason is amazing. He's absolutely a changed boy from last year.''

Heather felt a pleasant glow. ''Thank you. That's nice of you to say. He's been one of my best students. He just soaks up everything.'' She raised her head slightly and gave him a wicked smile. ''But I thought you were afraid he was working too hard?''

He shifted in his chair. ''Oh, please, don't bring that up. I was really reaching for that one.''

''And the thing about Ben Franklin?''

He grinned and pointed an accusing finger in her direction. ''Now the Ben Franklin bit was another matter entirely. Do you know what it's like to live in the same house with Ben Franklin for a week? And that kite. It's not easy to find a kite in town at this time of year.''

Uh-oh, I knew I'd hear about the kite, she thought. ''You can't believe how much good that little role-playing did him at school. It really brought him out of himself.''

''I know it did. I'm only kidding. I could even see a change in him at home after that. It seemed to build his confidence.''

''He's been working so hard.''

''I'm certain you've had a lot to do with that.'' He moved again uneasily in his chair. ''I probably shouldn't do this, but as long as I've come this far I might as well tell the whole truth. I've got another confession to make. That first day when I found out Jason was in your class, I even badgered Miss Nordway to move him. Did she tell you that?''

''No,'' Heather answered honestly. She kept to herself that she had overheard the confrontation between parent and principal.

''Luckily she ignored me on that score too. She's probably getting sick of seeing my face. I'm afraid I've made a pain of myself the last couple of years. What we doting parents make you teachers put up with.''

Heather smiled. ''I'd rather have parents who care than the ones who sit back and show no interest at all.''

''Very diplomatic. Have you thought of joining the foreign service?'' He took another sip of coffee. ''Seriously, you've never really had a time that you wanted to be something besides a teacher? Like an astronaut or a ballerina or something like that?''

There *was* something definitely different about him today, she decided. He could be positively charming when he wanted to be.

And Jess said the man had become almost a recluse! *He doesn't act much like a recluse to me,* she thought. She shook her head in response to his question. "No, I can't say that I ever wanted to do those things. I know where it all started too. Playing school. Did you ever play school when you were a kid?"

"Not that I can remember," he said. "I was too busy playing baseball and football."

"I did my share of that too, but we always seemed to play school in my neighborhood, and I was always the teacher. I guess I was just bossy or something." She laughed.

"I'll bet you made them toe the mark even then."

"As a matter of fact, I did," she admitted. "I think I might have come on a little strong. I can remember my mom used to have to break up some battles because I was always making one of my friends sit in the corner or something like that."

"I can imagine." He leaned forward. "Do you want another latte?"

Heather put her hand up. "Oh, no, one is my limit. That's all the caffeine I need for the day."

"I know what you mean." His eyes brightened as an idea suddenly struck him. "Do you have a few minutes?" he asked. "I'd like to show you something, if you have the time."

Heather checked her watch, wondering what he had on his mind. "Sure, why not? I've got a pile of papers waiting for me at home, but they're not going to run away."

"Good." He stood up and stepped around to her side of the table to help her with her chair. "My gallery is just a half block away. There's something I want you to see."

The two left the tiny coffee bar and headed up the street, Heather with a new nagging worry. This was Saturday and Becky Spooner would be working at the gallery. If she recognized Heather and said something, Marc would know Heather had been there before. Would that be so bad? Heather wondered. She could just pretend she had been aimlessly shopping that day. But knowing him he'd probably guess the truth—that her curiosity about him had gotten the better of her. A new thought struck her. What was she going to say if he asked her what she thought of those horrible paintings on display? Was that why he was taking her there? She didn't have long to worry, though.

They were at his gallery in a matter of seconds, and he held the door for her. Sure enough, Becky Spooner was at her place behind the desk by the front window, a paperback in hand. The woman looked up as they entered, and Heather watched for a sign of recognition, but there was none that she could detect. Marc introduced the two hastily and then led Heather toward the back of the gallery and the stairs. "Please don't look at any of these paintings," he cautioned. "I'm ashamed to take credit for them." *Hm,* Heather thought to herself, *so much for worry number two. I don't think he's going to ask for my opinion. He's already his own worst critic.*

They climbed the stairs, their footsteps echoing throughout the building. As she reached the top, movement in the far corner of the loft caught her attention. She was surprised to see Jason sitting at what looked to her like a potter's wheel. He had heard her come in downstairs, and now he was all business at the wheel. "Jason, is that you working so hard over there?"

He grinned shyly from his perch. "Hello, Miss DeLaney."

She went directly to him. "What are you working on?" she asked as she examined the glob of clay spinning on the wheel in front of him.

"A bowl," he said simply as he plunged a thumb into the clay and appeared to draw the sides of his bowl upward between a tiny thumb and forefinger.

Heather's jaw dropped in shock at the skill of his movement. It was obvious to her in an instant that he wasn't just playing at the wheel. He was truly working. Marc, standing to one side, smiled at her surprise. He could see that the boy was showing off for her benefit, but who could blame him? Oddly, Marc felt a strange boyish eagerness himself to show off his new painting to her. That was why he had asked her to the gallery on the spur of the moment, but he was perfectly content to let Jason get his due. He stepped over to a table by the railing, picked up a freshly fired vase, and handed it to her. "Jason has his work fired in the kiln next door at the co-op and displays some of his things there."

Heather handled the piece carefully, turning it slowly in her hands. "Why, Jason, this is beautiful. I had no idea you had such talent."

Jason concentrated at the wheel, doing his nine-year-old version of nonchalance. "Thanks," he said with a slight smile. Marc could tell by looking at the boy that he was about to explode with pride, and he saw just then the small thumb slice through the side of the bowl. He hoped Miss DeLaney hadn't noticed. The boy stole a quick glance up at his teacher to see if she had seen his mistake, and now it was his turn to gape. The bowl crashed in on itself, and the wheel came to a stop.

"I think he just noticed your hair," Marc whispered through a grin. "Hey, buddy, don't you like your teacher's new look?"

Still staring, the boy said quietly, "It's real nice."

Heather doubted she would ever hear a better compliment. "Why, thank you," she said. "I'll let you get back to work now. I know how hard it is to get something done with someone looking over your shoulder." She turned and took in the entire loft. "This is such a wonderful place to work. Plenty of room and light," she said, looking up at the skylight overhead.

"I wanted to show you what I was working on," Marc said as he gestured toward a large canvas resting on an easel by the railing of the loft. The canvas was facing away from them toward the front of the gallery, obviously to catch the light from the windows there. He stepped toward the work in progress, and she had no choice but to follow. Her insides did a sudden churn at the thought of being called upon to comment on one of his brooding paintings. She thought she had escaped all that. Two minutes ago she was certain Mr. Adams's sudden invitation to visit the gallery had been to see his son at work. Apparently not. She steeled herself as she stepped around the easel so her face wouldn't betray her feelings.

She let her eyes rest apprehensively on the beginnings of the painting, and she let out a rush of air in her surprise. "It's beautiful."

Marc was standing by the rail, watching her carefully. "It's not nearly finished," he said hastily.

"I know," she said, "but it has so much color, so much life." It was, in fact, the very same scene he had described to the class on the field trip. There was the shadow line with the detail of the craggy mountain that he had made them all see. The mountain itself was still sketchy, but Heather knew exactly what he intended. And the brightness where the sun had reflected off the mountain to create the line of shadow was there in all its brilliance, providing the contrast that he had talked about. The painting looked nothing like the drab things hanging downstairs. It reminded her of the work of his she had seen up at Timber Lodge. "How could you do this much so fast? You just got the idea yesterday, didn't you?"

He nodded. "Yes. I came down here right after the field trip and worked late last night." He looked toward Jason in the corner. The boy was starting afresh with his ruined bowl. "He's been a trouper. He worked on his pottery last night and then did some homework. I know he wasn't too happy to drag out early this morning for more of the same, but he didn't make one sound of complaint. To tell you the truth, I haven't worked in such a white heat like this in a long, long time, so I suppose he thought he'd better not spoil it. He's really something." He looked again toward his son with such love that Heather felt tears form in her eyes. "I'd better tear myself away this afternoon and take him to a movie. He deserves it."

Heather looked at the canvas again. "I can't tell you how impressed I am, Mr. Adams. This is really good. Now, you understand I'm not an art critic or anything, but I know what I like, and I like it."

The famous artist, like his son a moment ago, couldn't hide his pleasure at her words of praise. "Thank you. You can't imagine how glad I am to hear you say that."

Heather checked her watch. "Now I do have to get going. I'm keeping you two from your work, and I have that pile of papers at home calling my name." She nodded toward the painting. "Thanks for the sneak preview."

"My pleasure," he replied. "I'll be sure you see it when I'm finished."

"Oh, please, I'd like that." She waved toward Jason at his wheel. "See you on Monday, Jason. Thanks for the demonstration."

" 'Bye, Miss DeLaney," he called.

"I can find my way out," she said to Marc.

He followed her to the stairs. "Thanks for stopping by. Be sure to let me know if there's anything else I can do at school."

"Thank you, I will," Heather said brightly. She skipped down the stairs, nodded to Becky still buried in her book, and stepped outside. She had a happy feeling that she had just witnessed the return to life of a man who had been dead.

Chapter Thirteen

Jason squinted at the computer screen, his tongue clamped between his front teeth in his usual working mode. He read for the fifteenth time what he had written and moved the mouse with his small hand to make a final change.

"Are you about finished in there?"

"Yes, Dad, in a minute."

"You've been at it for two hours. We're going to be late for the movie if we don't hurry."

"Right," Jason called as he tapped the print key. He waited for the finished paper to slide out of the printer, snatched it, wrote something on it, and folded it carefully before stuffing it into his book bag. He saved his work and turned off the computer. Then he hurried to the front hall, where his dad was waiting.

"It's about time, buddy," Marc said as he pulled their jackets out of the closet. We're going to have to hurry."

"Sorry, Dad," Jason said as he caught the jacket tossed to him.

"What in the world were you working on in there, anyway?" Marc asked as he opened the door to the garage.

"Oh, nothin' much. Just something I'm writing."

Heather stood outside the door watching her class leave. It had been a hectic day, and she was almost as glad to hear the final bell as the kids were. She hoped she had heard the last of the comments on her hair. She had fielded a barrage of questions during the day. *Never again,* she decided. *Never again will I make a drastic change in my appearance during the school year. Save it for the summer.* She heaved a deep sigh of relief that the day was finally over and stepped back into her classroom. Jason was waiting patiently by her desk.

She brightened, the worry lines of the day fading. He could bring a smile to her face without even trying. She wondered how his last year's teacher could possibly have had trouble with the boy. "Jason, I didn't know you were still here. What can I do for you?" She swept around him and sat at the desk.

"I've got something to give you," he said quietly. He dug in his book bag and pulled out a sheet of paper. It was folded once, but it was badly wrinkled. He handed it to her. She smiled as she watched him, took the note, opened it, and read:

Dear Miss DeLaney,

Please come to dinner this Friday at 6:00. The address is 642 Deer Park Road. We hope you can come. Tell Jason if Friday is okay.

Sincerely yours,
Mr. Marc Adams

Heather was stunned. *Why wouldn't he use the telephone?* she wondered. *Such a strange little note.* She looked from the paper to Jason, who was standing by the desk watching her with those big brown eyes of his. "Well," she began slowly, "I guess Friday would be okay. Yes," she said with a sudden resolve, "tell your dad I would be happy to come for dinner."

She was rewarded for her acceptance by another of those rare, dazzling smiles of Jason's, the kind that seemed to change the whole appearance of the boy. "Thanks, Miss DeLaney. That's great." He turned and bolted for the door without another word, leaving her wondering what she had gotten herself into.

"You're moving along pretty fast, aren't you?" Shirley asked. She and Heather were on their way home. Heather had just turned her lights on. It was getting dark so early now, especially with the foothills towering on either side of the road. She had just told Shirley about the note and was almost wishing she hadn't when she heard the tone of her roommate's question.

"Why would you say that?" Heather asked.

"Oh, come on!" Shirley gave her roommate a look. "Wouldn't you say he's changed completely toward you? He's gone from wanting to have you fired and run out of town to having you practically recommended for teacher of the year."

"There's nothing personal in that," Heather insisted. "I've just been lucky enough to click with Jason, that's all. Mr. Adams is happy he's having a smooth year."

"So it's still Mr. Adams, is it?"

"Of course. I've always been very professional toward him." As she said it, she wondered to herself how professional their chat over café latte would be considered.

"Well, I don't know," Shirley said with a note of doubt in her voice, "you wouldn't consider dinner at his home just a teensy bit personal?"

"Not at all. It's just a home visit."

Shirley glanced quickly at her. "Uh-huh. A home visit. I haven't had many home visits that included dinner."

Jason blocked the door to the kitchen and put his shoulder against his dad's mid-section, pushing him back into the family room. "I'm fixing dinner tonight, Dad. You just watch the news or somethin'."

Marc let himself be eased backward. "What's the deal, buddy? You know we always do dinner as a team," he protested.

Jason had planted his feet and was pushing with all his might. Their big dog, Smoky, looked up from his spot by the fireplace. He bounded toward them, barking, ready for a little roughhousing. Marc stumbled over him and had to catch himself to keep from falling. "Not tonight," Jason said. "I've got a surprise, and you're not allowed in the kitchen till I say so." He pushed his dad toward the sofa in front of the television and settled him there. He turned on the set and handed him the remote. "Now you stay right there until I tell you to move." Smoky curled up at Marc's feet as if he were playing the role of enforcer.

Marc smiled at his son. "Whatever you say."

Jason dashed back to the kitchen. It was just after five-thirty. The water in a saucepan was boiling briskly, and he ripped open the package of hot dogs he had set out and dumped them in the water. He pulled open a cupboard door and stretched to reach the plates. He carried three of them to the table in the eating area adjoining the kitchen and arranged them carefully. He thought about using the fancy dining room where they never ate anymore, but he knew his dad would wonder about that. The hiss of water boiling over sent him scurrying again to the stove. The saucepan filled with hot dogs was splashing over the hot burner. He turned the burner down and slid the pan to one side to wait until the temperature cooled.

"Everything all right out there?" Marc called.

"Yes, Dad, everything's fine." He pulled open the door of the built-in pantry and scanned the rows of cans until he found the one he wanted. Pork and beans. He pulled it out, climbed the step stool by the counter, and fitted the can into the electric can opener. He poured the contents into a second pan, put it next to his hot dogs, and clicked on the burner.

Next, he returned to the pantry and pulled out a large unopened bag of potato chips. He ripped the bag, pulled a bowl out of a cupboard, and dumped the chips in. He set the bowl carefully in the center of the table. Then it was back to the pantry, this time for a package of hot dog buns. He headed for the table, tearing the package open as he went. He stood at the table for a moment thinking and then arranged three buns on each plate.

He stood in the middle of the kitchen trying to remember if he had everything on his menu. He made a face. He wanted to make coffee, but he had no idea how to do that. With a smile, he decided on an alternative. He pulled the orange juice pitcher from the refrigerator and poured three large glasses of juice. He made three trips to the table, carrying each glass carefully. While he was putting the juice back, he noticed the ketchup, mustard, and relish, which he transported to his table. He took a deep breath and mopped his brow. He peeked in the two pans and decided the contents were bubbling at an acceptable rate. He looked at the clock on the stove. It was five forty-five. He went back to the family room.

"Dad, are you going to change your clothes?"

Marc was stretched out on the sofa, engrossed in a news story on the screen. Smoky was sleeping on the floor by his side. Marc looked up. "What's that?"

Jason was standing at the kitchen door. ''I said why don't you change your clothes?''

Marc looked down at himself. He was wearing dark blue sweatpants and a purple sweatshirt, its front speckled with various hues of oil paint—his favorite painting outfit. ''What's wrong with this?''

''Daaad!'' Jason groaned. ''It looks gross.''

''I never heard you complain about it before.''

''Please!'' the boy pleaded.

''Oh, all right. What's the big deal, anyway?'' He hauled himself off the sofa and headed for the kitchen. ''What's for dinner?''

Jason blocked his way. ''Just never mind. It's a surprise.''

Marc stuck his head through the door and sniffed. ''I smell hot dogs and baked beans. Right?''

Jason didn't answer. He pushed his dad away from the doorway and toward the stairs.

''You sure are mighty secretive tonight,'' Marc called as he climbed the stairs. He came down minutes later in dark slacks and a pullover sweater. He had slipped into a pair of loafers. ''Can I come to the table now?'' he called.

''No, not yet. I'll call you when it's time.''

Marc returned to the sofa with a wide grin on his face. *I wonder what brought this all about?* he thought. *Probably something they're doing in school,* he guessed.

Meanwhile, back in the kitchen, Jason was nearing the moment of truth. He hadn't planned far enough in advance to know what he was going to do when Miss DeLaney showed up at the door. How he could make it appear that his dad had invited her he wasn't exactly sure. And what would his dad do? he wondered. He checked the clock. It was nearly six o'clock. She was always on time, and as if to confirm his confidence in her, the doorbell rang. Smoky sat up and barked. ''I'll get it, Dad,'' Jason called as he raced from the kitchen, just beating the big dog to the door.

Marc was off of the sofa and halfway to the entryway when Jason pulled the door open. He could hear the boy say hello to someone, and the returned greeting was familiar. Then as the door swung wider, he saw her, nearly at the same time the voice registered in his memory. She was just about the last person he expected to see at his front door. She was wearing a maroon quilted coat against the mountain chill and a beige knitted hat to protect her new short hair. *Now what in the world is she doing here?* he wondered.

Heather turned toward him then and smiled. "Hello, Mr. Adams. This was very nice of you." She noticed a strange look on his face, a mixture of surprise and confusion that might not have caught her attention on anyone else. But with this man who always seemed so controlled and in charge, the look was unmistakable.

Marc glanced from Miss DeLaney to his son. He could see that Jason was making himself just a little too busy—slamming the door with a great flourish and then taking his teacher's coat with more attention than he had ever shown to anyone that Marc could ever remember. *He's been up to something,* Marc decided. He began to put things together. All that rattling about in the kitchen. The business about dressing up. And ever since he'd come home from school the little guy had been as nervous as a first-time skier at the top of the slope. Now it all made sense. He finally found his voice. "We're very glad you could come. Jason's in charge tonight, isn't that right?" Father and son exchanged a look. "He's been working like a regular chef."

Jason hurried to the front closet to hang Miss DeLaney's coat. He breathed a sigh of relief. *So far, so good.*

Smoky was circling the group. "What a beautiful Lab," Heather observed. "What's his name?"

Jason had finally reached the rod with the hanger. "Smoky," he said as he closed the door.

Heather bent over. "Hello, Smoky. How are you, boy?" She held her hand out to the dog, and he came obediently to her. She cradled his head in her two hands and rubbed his ears. "Good dog. Oh, you're such a nice doggy, aren't you?" she sang to him.

"I guarantee you've made a friend for life. Are you ready for us out in the kitchen, buddy?" Marc asked.

"Wait till I put the stuff on the table," Jason answered as he backed toward the kitchen. He gave his dad a look that said more than words ever could. It said *Thanks for not giving me away and please, please, please keep playing along.*

"Let's wait in the great room," Marc said, and he turned to lead the way. Heather touched his arm, and he turned toward her.

She said quietly, almost whispering because she didn't want Jason to hear, "You didn't know a thing about this, did you?"

His smile was all the answer she needed. "The truth? I didn't have a clue."

Her face flushed. "I'm sorry. I should have known. Maybe I'd better go."

Marc turned toward her, alarmed, remembering the "look" Jason had given him on the way to the kitchen. "No, you can't do that. It would break his heart. He's been working on this dinner for hours. Wouldn't let me near the kitchen."

"But it's such an imposition," she protested.

"Not at all. This is good for him. He needs to work on his social skills a little. You'd better prepare yourself, though. I think it's beans and hot dogs."

She laughed. "Two of my favorites."

"Here, let me get the lights," Marc said. He clicked a switch and a row of spots came on overhead in the vaulted ceiling. She had caught just a glimpse of this room from the front door. She stopped now and looked about her. "What a beautiful home you have."

Heather saw a massive stone fireplace at one end, its light stone extending all the way to the ceiling. Windows on either side of the fireplace also soared to the ceiling. She walked close to one of them and peered out. She could see spots of light in the distance and the murky shapes of trees and hills. She turned. "I'll bet you have a beautiful view from here."

"Big Bear is just off to your right. It *is* beautiful, especially in early morning and just at sunset."

"I can imagine," Heather said as she stood before the window, trying to make out the shapes in the distance. She turned slowly, taking in the room. The tasteful furniture was arranged carefully in a semicircle around the fireplace. Heather could only guess that the house had not been changed much since Mrs. Adams's death. *Neat as a pin,* she noted. *They probably have a cleaning service,* she thought, *but still—not bad for a man.* She knew that wasn't being fair, but she couldn't help it. She was remembering the time she and her mother went away for a week to visit an aunt in Michigan and left her dad and brother alone. The place looked like a candidate for federal disaster aid when they got back, and that was in a week's time. She wondered if Jason had made a special effort at cleanup tonight.

She looked up suddenly and saw Mr. Adams watching her. "We don't use this room much," he said, and she knew then he had been reading her mind. She felt very much like an intruder at that moment.

He motioned her to a chair and sat across from her. Smoky stood by her chair as she sat down and then sat himself, laying his head against her leg. Marc stared at the dog in amusement. "Smoky, what's wrong with you? I'm sorry, he usually doesn't act like that." He started up out of his chair. "I'll put him in the garage."

"No, he's fine, really. He just wants his ears scratched." She patted the big head and scratched behind each ear. "Don't you, boy? Sure. You're a good dog, aren't you?" Smoky looked contentedly over at Marc, for all the world like a child safely on Grandma's lap daring Mom or Dad to make him behave.

Marc did his best to ignore the dog. "I told you what a hit you've made with Jason. I guarantee you he would never dream of doing anything like this for one of his other teachers. How did he set it up, anyway?"

"He gave me an invitation, all very formal. It was supposedly from you. He'd done it on the computer." She raised an eyebrow and cleared her throat. "Uh, I guess I should tell you your name was signed to it."

"Uh-oh," he said. "I'll have to talk to him about that. He's getting a little too frisky with that computer." He knitted his brow. "One thing I'm curious about. What gave me away? How did you know I wasn't in on this whole thing? I thought I was pretty smooth."

She laughed. "You recovered nicely, I must admit. But that first reaction." Now she laughed again, only this time it was more of a giggle. It made him laugh to hear her. "I'm sorry," she went on, "I shouldn't laugh, but you should have seen the look on your face when you saw me at the door. I knew you weren't expecting me. I hope you don't play poker."

Jason was busy in the kitchen. He poured the steaming beans into a bowl and set it on the table. Next, he speared the hot dogs with a fork and placed them on a platter. This he also set on his table. He was ready. He went to the doorway and looked in. His dad and Miss DeLaney were talking quietly. He watched them for a minute, not wanting to interrupt, but he knew his dinner was getting cold. ''Time to eat,'' he sang. They both looked toward him and stood up.

''We're coming,'' Marc announced. ''We're both starved, so there'd better be plenty.''

Heather had years of experience at treating young people seriously when what they were doing might tempt her to smile or, worse yet, laugh out loud. All elementary teachers—at least the good ones, anyway—were able to do that, she knew. They learned to prepare themselves for the unexpected because the unexpected usually happened. Hardly a day went by that one of her fourth graders didn't do something or say something in class that would make her howl with laughter if she weren't practically biting her cheek to keep a straight face.

Why just yesterday during share time, little Daren McCloud brought his grandfather's full set of dentures floating in a pint jar of water. He was giving an important lesson about brushing after meals, but it was all lost on Heather because she was worrying about the boy's grandfather and how he was managing without his teeth. And she couldn't help wondering if Grandpa McCloud knew where those teeth had disappeared to. She remembered when she was a kid, she and her best friend, Jaimie, used to present plays for her mom and dad. They were horrible, contrived things that they rehearsed in all earnestness and presented badly with much fanfare and usually with old Stuff, the dog, stealing the show. But her mom and dad always watched from start to finish and applauded loudly at the curtain even when the play disintegrated in midscene. She took her cue from them in dealing with youngsters.

But what awaited them in the kitchen nearly got the best of her. It took all of that built-in and acquired sensitivity of hers to deal with those three hot dog buns placed neatly on each plate. But she pulled it off, and she noticed that Mr. Adams did too, but he needed a quick drink of water to overcome a sudden coughing attack.

In fact, dinner went off without a hitch. She could manage

only two of her allotted hot dogs, though. She watched in amusement at Jason's efforts to play host. Over their beans and hot dogs and potato chips, the three talked about school mostly, with some sports thrown in, especially the prospects of the Denver Broncos in the upcoming playoffs. And naturally skiing worked its way into their conversation. The snow base was building at Bear Claw, but even now the skiing was acceptable. Father and son had tried the slopes several times, but Heather was ashamed to admit she hadn't dug her skis out of the closet yet. She claimed the demands of the new school year as her excuse. As Heather finished the last of her hot dog, Jason ran for the refrigerator. He had even planned ahead for dessert—a Popsicle for each of them, and they got to choose their flavor. When they were finished, he slid out of his chair and began clearing the table.

Heather leaned back in her chair. "That was delicious, Jason. Thank you so much for inviting me." He gave a quick look from her to his dad, afraid his deception had been found out.

But Marc rescued him. "We thought you deserved a break from all that school food," he said with a wink at Heather that Jason missed. Marc knew he would have to talk with his son about the business of the invitation, but that could wait until later. And besides, the evening had been a good one despite its surprise start. He actually wished he'd thought of it himself.

Heather looked at her watch. "I hate to eat and run, but I should be going. I have a lot of work to do."

Marc studied her with a faint smile on his face. "On a Friday night?"

"I don't like to have it hanging over my head," she explained. "If I get it done right away Friday night or early Saturday, then I have the rest of the weekend to enjoy."

He shook his head. "I don't know how you can do that. If I can put it off until tomorrow, that's what I do, I'm afraid. Not a very good philosophy for an artist who works with a deadline."

Jason was putting the last of the dishes in the dishwasher. "Dad, can I show Miss DeLaney our new computer?"

"Sure, son, if she has the time."

The boy looked at her expectantly. She nodded. "All right. I don't have to go right this minute."

He led the way out of the kitchen, through the great room, and down a hallway into a room at its end that Heather guessed was a solarium or a studio. He clicked on the light. Mr. Adams and Smoky were right at her heels again.

This room hadn't much furniture. There was a large oak computer desk at one end, and that was where Jason was heading. Along with that one desk, there were several pieces of exercise equipment and what looked like an easel in the middle of the room shrouded under a dark green cloth. She followed Jason to the computer; he had already clicked it on. She watched over his shoulder as he took her through the rudiments of the programs, including a game that he wanted her to play. She sat at the desk and tried her hand, posting a reasonable score for a beginner. She relinquished the chair to Jason and watched him show off his skills on the same game.

"I'm afraid you're too good for me," she said, stepping away from the desk. "Can you beat him, Mr. Adams?"

"Not really. I think he plays off to me to keep me interested."

"No, I don't, Dad," Jason said between moves. "You're not too bad for an old person."

Marc laughed. "Am I supposed to take that as a compliment or what?"

Heather smiled at the two. She looked about her. She saw windows again, this time lining one long wall. "I'll bet there's another beautiful view out there."

"Yes, but not as spectacular as the one from the great room. You can see the foothills from this side. I think in some ways they're more beautiful, though. There's more color, especially at the right time of the year."

She had strolled slowly toward the shrouded easel. "So you paint here? There must be plenty of light."

Marc followed her. He had folded his arms across his chest, and his fingers tapped nervously against his upper arms. "Oh, I do a little work here."

"Uh-uh!" Jason said unexpectedly from his place in front of the computer. His right hand was moving the mouse at lightning speed on its pad, but he was still listening to them.

"How do you know so much?" Marc asked, attempting an offhand manner that didn't quite work.

"Aw, Dad, I haven't seen you do anything in here since Mom

died,'' the boy said matter-of-factly, the dull tone of his voice reflecting his involvement in the game.

There was an awkward silence. Heather was standing by the covered easel. ''It looks like you have something started here,'' she said, trying to get through the uncomfortable moment.

''Don't touch that,'' Marc blurted as he made a sudden step toward the easel.

Startled, Heather stepped quickly away from the painting as if she had gotten too close to a hot stove. ''I wasn't going to.''

''I'm sorry. I didn't mean to startle you. It's just that it's not very good, and I don't want anyone to see it.'' He adjusted the cover almost reverently.

''It's just some dumb old garden,'' Jason said from his place.

''He's always my worst critic,'' Marc said with a forced laugh.

Heather knew she had stumbled where she didn't belong. She examined her watch. ''I really must be going if I have any hope of getting any work done tonight.'' She started for the door. ''How many points do you have now, Jason?''

''Fifty-seven thousand,'' he answered.

''Fifty-seven thousand! That's twice as many as I had.''

''And I still have three rockets left.''

''You're too good for me. I'll see you on Monday. Now don't spend all weekend on that game.'' She couldn't resist playing the teacher. ''Remember, we have a big geography test Monday.''

''I won't forget.''

''Thanks for dinner.''

''Sure. 'Bye, Miss DeLaney,'' he called as she left the room and headed back down the hall toward the front door, Mr. Adams and Smoky trailing behind.

Marc got her coat and held it for her. He was upset with himself for what had just happened. He was certain his blunder had ruined the evening. ''I'm sorry I barked at you in there. He's right, you know. It is just a dumb old garden, and I can't seem to get it right. I should throw the thing out.''

Heather slipped her arms in the sleeves of her coat. She knew there was more to what was hidden under that shroud than a dumb old garden, but it was none of her business. But she certainly hadn't expected such a reaction from just standing near the easel. She turned around. "Oh, don't do that, Mr. Adams. Keep at it. You'll get it."

"Maybe someday." He brightened. "Thank you so much for coming. I know it meant a lot to Jason. He doesn't act like it in there, but I know it did. That game seems to turn him into some kind of a zombie."

Heather laughed. "I think it's a pretty common affliction for kids his age. Well, thanks for asking me." She raised an eyebrow. "On second thought, I guess you didn't have any part in that, did you?" She laid a hand on his arm. "Now, don't be too hard on him. He was so cute."

He put his hand on the doorknob. "Whatever you say. You're the teacher. Could I ask a big favor? Would it be possible for you to call me Marc? This Mr. Adams business sounds too formal for me. Does that break any school rule or anything?"

Heather laughed. "None that I know of. Okay, Marc it is, but now you have to call me Heather."

He rolled his eyes. "I don't know. That must be against some school rule."

"I promise I won't tell."

"Heather," he said as if trying the name for the first time. "What a pretty name. Have you seen the mountain heather of Ireland?"

"I haven't had the pleasure of going there yet, but someday I hope to."

"Such beautiful color against all that green of the Emerald Isle. You are well named."

She knew her face reddened at the compliment, but she was thankful it wasn't obvious in the shadows of the front hall. "Why, thank you. Thank you again for a wonderful evening." She tugged her collar up around her neck and went out into the chill mountain air.

Heather was still up working at the dining-room table when Shirley got home from her date with Erik. They had gone to a late movie. He came in for a promised dish of ice cream, and Heather had to move her bulletin board cutout figures to one side to make room.

Shirley was dishing the ice cream. "You want some, don't you, Heath?"

"Sure, why not? I am a little hungry, to tell you the truth."

Shirley whirled, the ice-cream scoop poised in midair. "Where is my brain tonight? I forgot to ask you about dinner." Aside, she said to Erik, "She was invited to dinner at the house of one of her students. You know Marc Adams, the artist? We were talking about him that one night at Timber Lodge." Erik nodded. "So tell us all about it."

"Well, for starters, remember I wondered if Marc knew about the invitation? He didn't."

Shirley turned again. "You're kidding! How did the little guy pull that off?"

"He just didn't tell his dad. He fixed dinner all by himself."

"Really?" Shirley put the bowls of ice cream on the table and went to the refrigerator for topping. "What did you have to eat?"

"Hot dogs and beans and potato chips. And a Popsicle for dessert."

Shirley set a jar of chocolate sauce and a jar of caramel sauce in the middle of the table. "Isn't that cute?" She poked Erik on the arm. "Isn't that sweet, Erik?"

"Uh-huh, wieners and beans and crisps. He knows his American basic food groups," he proclaimed as he poured chocolate on his ice cream.

"Oh, you," Shirley said in mock anger. "You don't seem to have any trouble choking down our junk food." She sat and pulled her bowl of ice cream toward her. "So what happened when you showed up? Didn't Mr. Adams about lose it or what?"

Heather laughed. "It was close, but he handled things pretty well. I might not have suspected he didn't know if it hadn't been for the look on his face when he first saw me. But he got himself under control right away and went along with it."

"What could he do?" Erik observed. "Even an American would not throw a pretty girl out into the street."

Shirley gave him a disgusted look. "I must say, you're such a romantic." She turned to her roommate again. "So how did the evening go?"

"Oh, fine. I wasn't there very long, really. That house is absolutely gorgeous."

"Tell me, tell me. What's it like? It looks beautiful from the outside. All that wood and glass."

"Well, it's more of the same inside. Nice big living room, or great room as Marc calls it, and a huge kitchen."

Shirley had her head cocked to one side. "Excuse me, did I hear right? Is it Marc now?"

Heather colored slightly. "It's no big thing. He asked me to call him Marc just before I came home."

Shirley arched her eyebrows. "Uh-huh. Who was it who told me how professional this relationship was? All of a sudden it doesn't sound so professional."

"Don't make a . . . how do you say it? . . . federal case out of it," Erik said as he looked up from his ice cream. "It's just a name."

"Right," Heather agreed, thankful, for a change, for one of Erik's remarks. Anything to get Shirley off her case.

And it worked. Shirley's eyes suddenly brightened at the thought of something. "Erik, remember what we said we were going to ask Heather, and we won't take no for an answer?"

Erik nodded and he turned his light blue eyes on Heather. "Yes, you are going skiing with us tomorrow. In the afternoon. I have lessons in the morning but nothing in the afternoon. A free lift ticket, so you cannot say no."

"Please?" Shirley pleaded. "You said you'd go. And don't try to tell us you've got too much work to do because we aren't buying it. Right, Erik?"

"Right," he said. "Or I must assume that you are a true flatlander who does not know a ski pole from a hockey stick."

"Sounds to me like a challenge," Heather said as she stuck her chin out at the pair. "Okay, okay, you win. But it's been so long I may *not* know a ski pole from a hockey stick. I probably should sign up for your morning lessons."

"I only have room in my class for fat old ladies," he said as he studied her across the table. "And I am sorry, but you don't qualify."

Heather laughed. "Well, thank goodness for that." She stood and gathered up her cutout figures. "Now, if you two will excuse me, I'm going to bed. I have to get up early to have my skis waxed."

Chapter Fourteen

Shirley slipped the car into one of the last remaining parking spaces, far from the ski lodge, and the two got out and began to remove their skis from the ski rack. Shirley was enclosed head to foot in her brand-new ski clothes, the brightest yellow outfit Heather had ever seen. In fact, when her roommate had appeared in the living room dressed for their outing, Heather had shielded her eyes in a mocking gesture at the brilliance of the outfit. "Listen," Shirley had explained, "if an avalanche catches me, I want the searchers to be able to see me a mile away." Heather was wearing a kelly green affair that was only slightly less eye-catching. It was two years old now, but Heather was relieved to discover that it still fit like a glove—and a surgical glove at that.

The two women shouldered their skis and began the long trudge across the parking lot to the lodge. Heather looked about her, ever mindful of her pledge to herself to enjoy the mountains to the fullest. It was an easy pledge to keep in a place like this and on a day like this. The mountains in front of her formed a natural bowl with the lodge at its center. The slopes that made up the base of those mountains had been groomed into the various ski runs of Bear Claw. She already knew from past experience that some of those runs were treacherous, demanding the skill of truly expert skiers, while others were tamer, drawing the vast majority of thrill seekers, and a few were even pussycats, the beginner slopes.

It was here on one of those bunny slopes where she had cut her teeth on the sport. Now she spent most of her time on the greens and the blues, venturing occasionally up to the blacks when she was looking for more excitement. She even tried a black diamond once in a while when she was feeling particularly daring. She would spend more time on those demanding runs if she skied more often, she decided.

The day couldn't have been more perfect. It was chilly, in fact even cold at this altitude, but the sun was bright with not a cloud overhead. It had snowed up here just last night, six inches, according to the local radio report, and the base was building nicely. Today they could expect a powder under their skis that would give them good speed and control.

Heather breathed deeply. "This is the life!" she practically shouted.

"You said it!" Shirley answered with feeling. "Now aren't you ashamed we practically had to drag you up here? We should be doing this every day. My gosh, it's only three miles from where we live. Think of the people who would kill to be that close."

"You're absolutely right," Heather said with a smile. "Let's become ski bums."

"I'd go for that," Shirley agreed. "Hey, there's Erik, and right on time, for a change."

Erik was standing by the gate to the lift, watching their approach. "Welcome," he announced as they came closer, "to the loveliest ladies on the slopes today."

"Why, thank you, Erik," Shirley gushed. "Doesn't he say the nicest things?"

"Once in a while he does," Heather said with a smile.

Erik wagged a finger at her. "You have wounded me deeply. And where were you this morning? You were not at my morning lesson."

"Now wait just a minute," Heather said, pretending injury, "you said your morning lesson was for fat old women."

"S!" he said with a finger to his lips. "Oh, please, don't say such things where others may hear. Erik will be skiing the avalanche patrol if anyone should hear those words." His voice became louder. "All my students this morning were Hollywood beauty queens who only wanted to know the finer points of slalom turns."

"I'll bet," Shirley said, and the two women laughed.

He handed them their lift tickets. "Now, let's get started. I am anxious to see the moves of Miss Flatlander here. Shall we start on a black diamond to get ourselves limbered?''

"No, we will not start on a black diamond," Heather shot back. "This is my first time out this year, remember. I'm thinking of a green slope or maybe a blue." She turned to Shirley. "I just knew it. This is going to be like going driving with a driving instructor. I won't be able to do anything with *him* watching me."

Shirley smiled. "Don't worry. I'll keep him out of your face." She turned to Erik. "Listen, buster, you're supposed to be watching me. Okay?"

He bowed slightly toward her. "Your beauty shines like the sun. I cannot take my eyes from you."

"Well, that's more like it," she said smugly.

Heather was making a show of inspecting her skis, but her eyes sparkled in amusement. "Are you sure it's her beauty that shines like the sun, or is it that outfit she's wearing?"

Shirley stamped a ski boot. "Whose side are you on, anyway?"

"I'm sorry. I couldn't resist."

"Ladies, ladies, I hate when you fight over me like this." They both reached for handfuls of snow to pelt him with, and he held up his hands in surrender. "Take your anger out on the mountain. She is waiting," he said, pointing over his shoulder in the direction of Big Bear. "Are we ready?" He extended his arm in an exaggerated flourish, inviting them through the gate. The two snapped on their skis, readied their poles, and shuffled toward the lift with Erik following behind. "Oh, Heather, your friend Marc Adams and his little boy are here today," he remarked casually.

Heather turned, a mix of surprise and pleasure showing on her face. "Really?" she asked.

"Yes, I saw them get on the lift before you came."

Not more than five minutes later Heather was hundreds of feet in the air with her skis dangling below her as the swaying chair she was on moved steadily upward toward the first run. She could feel a fluttering in her stomach that she recognized as a mix of excitement and just a little fear. She always felt like this before every run, more so if she hadn't skied for a while. She looked about her. The view was spectacular. The mountains towered above, their peaks and crags and vertical stretches showing dark against the snow that clung wherever it could. Then on both sides of her and above were the many runs, some slicing through stands of pines still decorated with last night's snow, and others wide and gently sloping down the base of the mountain. From where she sat, the snow looked fluffy and soft and feathery. *It never feels that way when you fall,* she thought. She could see hundreds of skiers racing down the many runs. They grew smaller and smaller as she climbed higher and higher, but she could still make out the yellows and reds and blues and greens of their outfits.

She let her skis touch and slid off the chair when she reached the top. She joined Erik and Shirley as they moved toward the beginning of the run. She pulled her goggles down and looked to see if the other two were ready. Shirley nodded. Heather pushed with her poles to move to the edge. She looked ahead. The wide white path stretched beyond her, making a gentle turn to the left. She could see the sun glinting off the windows of the lodge far below. She waved to the two behind her. ''Last one to the bottom's a rotten egg,'' she shouted as she pushed off with her poles. Shirley shouted something back, but Heather missed her words with the sudden rush of air past her ears.

She felt a moment's loss of control, that awful feeling that she was going to go straight down the mountainside at ever-increasing speed until she ran into who knew what at the bottom, but she flexed her knees and made a gentle turn to the right, beginning a series of parallel runs that would keep her speed under control. She was aware of the blur of those around her. Some were going faster than she and slipped quickly by her. Others she passed, always keeping alert for any falls on their part. *Skiing would be a lot easier if it weren't for all these other crazy people,* she thought with a grin.

And then she let herself revel in the exhilaration that had sent her back to the top of the bunny slopes after that first awkward run so many years ago and that had brought her back to Bear Claw time and time again. She knew everyone around her was feeling the same thing. It was the speed, the sound of the snow under her skis, the smell of the pines, the feeling of control, the turns, the wind against her face. It was all those things and more that she couldn't describe. And then it was over. She made a neat little turn to slow herself, bounced with her knees, and came to a stop. She pushed with her poles and glided in the direction of the lift, pulling off her goggles to check behind for Erik and Shirley.

They pulled in just then, Erik doing a little hotdogging with a turn at the last that threw a shower of snow.

"Show-off!" she shouted at him with a wide smile as they poled toward her.

He did a low bow in her direction. "From now on there will be no more talk of Miss Flatlander. You are very good. You look like a student of the great Erik Sorenson."

Heather laughed. "I think I'll take that as a compliment." She took a deep breath. "That was so much fun."

"Miss DeLaney!" a voice called.

Heather looked toward the lift. Jason and his dad were in line to get on, and the boy was waving wildly. When she saw him and waved back, Marc gave a short wave of his own. "There they are," Heather said.

"Yes, there they are," Shirley repeated with a raise of her eyebrow.

"Shall we go again?" Heather asked as she moved toward the lift line.

"That's what we came for," Shirley said as she fell in behind her roommate.

Marc and Jason were waiting at the top when Heather glided off the lift. "Miss DeLaney, will you ski down with us? Please?" the boy begged.

"All right, but don't go too fast for me."

Marc nodded. "Hello, Heather," he said quietly. He still felt strangely awkward using her name, especially around his son. "We saw the last part of your run. Jason recognized you when you were still way up there." He pointed up the mountain. "You're very good."

"Why, thank you. I can hold my own on the greens and blues, but don't get me up on the blacks." Heather looked around for Shirley and Erik. They were standing to one side, waiting. "Marc, I'd like you to meet my roommate, Shirley Merrill. She teaches first grade at Keats. Shirley, this is Marc Adams." The two nodded and said hello. "And this is her friend, Erik Sorenson. Erik, this is Marc Adams."

"Don't I know you?" Marc asked.

"I am the director of skiing here," Erik replied in his formal way.

"Of course. I see you on the mountain all the time."

"And," Heather broke in again, "this is my student Jason Adams. Miss Merrill and Mr. Sorenson." Jason beamed at not being left out.

"I have seen you ski, young man," said Erik very seriously. "Your fundamentals are very sound."

"I think that means he thinks you're a good skier," Heather translated.

"Heath," Shirley interrupted, "I hate to break this up, but I'm getting cold. We're going on up to another level. You want to come?"

"I think I'll try this one again until I get a little more comfortable. Anyway, I promised Jason I'd ski down with him."

"Right," Shirley said with just a slight questioning tone in her voice that only Heather heard. "Well, we'll catch up with you later." With that, she and Erik moved off toward the lift that would take them higher.

The trio glided slowly toward the starting point. They busied themselves getting their goggles in place, and Heather adjusted her stocking cap. Marc looked over at her before he glanced back at his son. "You ready to start us out, Jace?"

That was all the signal the boy needed. He was gone in a flash, streaking down the run. Heather shoved hard with her poles to try to keep up, but she found it impossible to catch the boy. He was taking a straighter and faster course down the mountainside, and she had no idea if he was showing off for her benefit or if that was his usual skiing style. She was vaguely aware that Marc was skiing near her, but she had no chance of catching Jason. He was watching her with a huge grin on his freckled face as she came to the bottom. Her skis slipped out from under her as she made a little turn to stop, and she plopped into the soft snow near him just as Marc joined them in a spray of snow. He reached

out a gloved hand to pull her up. "You guys are slow," Jason
said in a taunting voice. "Can we go again? Please?" he begged.

Heather looked at Marc. "Does he ever stop?"

"He could go like that all day long."

They did two more runs, both on blues, but each a different
blue. Heather had lost sight of Erik and Shirley, though she
thought she saw Shirley's bright yellow outfit far below her as
they were on the lift the last time up. When they finished the
second blue, Jason raced ahead to get in line at the lift, but
Heather lagged behind. "I've got to take a break," she said to
Marc. "You two go ahead without me on this next one."

"I'm getting a little winded myself," he admitted. "Jason!"
he shouted. The boy turned. "Let's stop for a few minutes. We
can get something to drink."

Jason frowned. "Do we hafta?"

"Yes, we all need a break."

The three moved to one side and snapped their skis off. They
made their way to the entrance of the lodge, walking almost
robotlike with the suddenly strange sensation of having to rely
on mere feet again. They stowed their skis and poles in one of
the racks before they pushed their way through the crowd at the
door. Heather could see there was a long line at the cafeteria to
one side of the rough-beamed, high-ceilinged room. She knew
the cafeteria was the only place to get a quick snack. There was
a dining room in another part of the lodge, but the service was
slow and the food expensive. "Why don't you two grab that table
over there," Marc said, pointing, "and I'll get us something.
Coke? Is that okay?" Heather and Jason nodded.

"Can I have a hamburger, Dad?" Jason asked just as Marc
turned to get in line. He looked back.

"Sure. How about you, Heather?"

"Mm, that does sound good. I ate before I came, but I'm
starved."

"Skiing takes a lot out of you. Okay, three burgers and three
Cokes. Is that all?"

Heather made her way to the table Marc had spotted. There
weren't many empty ones, but the good thing about skiing, she
knew, was that everyone was in such a hurry to get back to the
slopes that tables opened up quickly. She sat and pulled off her

stocking cap, running her hand through her tangled hair. Now she was grateful for the short haircut. "You're quite a skier," she said to Jason, who was sitting across from her at the tiny table. "Have you been skiing a long time?"

He nodded. "My mom took me to lessons on the bunny slope when I was five years old, I think. I kind of forget exactly, but it was a long time ago."

Heather smiled at a nine-year-old's version of a long time. "No wonder you're so good if you've been at it that long."

He folded his hands in front of him on the table. "We used to come here all the time before my baby sister got born. After that, Mom didn't ski. She'd come with the baby and watch me and Dad."

"What was your sister's name?"

"Karrie."

"Oh, that's such a pretty name."

He smiled and studied her with those big brown eyes of his. "Do you like my dad?"

Heather was surprised by his question, but she knew she shouldn't be. She was used to hearing her students say whatever came to their minds without thinking. She could feel her face redden, and she fought to overcome the feeling. "I think he's very nice," she said simply.

"He likes you too. I can tell. He calls you by your first name instead of Miss DeLaney."

The first-name thing comes back to haunt me already, she thought. She didn't know quite what to say, but she needn't have worried. It was obvious Jason wasn't expecting her to say anything anyway. He was just sitting there, quietly studying her across the table. She knew that hearing a teacher's first name could be a shock for an elementary student. After all, the teachers in school were all very careful to use Mr. or Miss or Mrs. to refer to each other when students were around. She remembered once when she was in third grade, or it might have been fourth, she wasn't sure. One of the boys found out the teacher's name was Harriet, and the kids called her Harriet behind her back for the rest of the year. The boys, mostly, but Heather knew she had done it a time or two herself. Strange how such a simple thing seemed so shocking to her at the time. As if teachers weren't expected to have first names. She finally found her voice. "That's because we're friends. Your dad calls the two women who work in his gallery by their first names, doesn't he?"

"You mean Doris and Becky? Yeah."

"That's because they're friends of his and he knows them real well."

"I call them Doris and Becky too. So can I call you Heather too, like my dad does?"

Heather could feel beads of perspiration on her forehead, and it wasn't because this big barn of a cafeteria was too warm. "There's a difference. I'm your teacher and you call me Miss DeLaney to show respect."

"Oh," he said simply, and Heather could see him slowly turn that information around in his head. She hoped that was the end of that topic.

"If you married my dad, would I still have to call you Miss DeLaney?"

Marc appeared out of nowhere just then with an orange tray loaded with burgers and Cokes, saving Heather from that question. She could have kissed him for his good timing, but then that would have caused more questions. He served each of them and plopped a huge cardboard dish of curly fries in the middle of the table. He set the empty tray on a table nearby and sat down. "I couldn't pass up those fries when I saw them. Any objections?"

"No way, Dad," Jason said. He already had the wrapper off his burger and was preparing to bite in.

"So what have you two been talking about?" Marc asked, looking from one to the other.

"Oh, this and that," Heather volunteered. She could see across the table that Jason wanted to say something, but his mouth was full of burger. He chewed quickly and swallowed. She held her breath, waiting for what he was going to come out with.

"Dad, don'tcha think Miss DeLaney is a better skier than Mom?"

Heather could see a cloud pass over Marc's face. *Jason is loaded with the shockers today,* she thought. "I hadn't really thought about it," he said. "Yes, I guess she is."

''Me too. She's almost as good as you are, don'tcha think, Dad?''

''She just might be. But we'll take her up to our favorite blue and see how she does there.''

''You mean Porkypine, through all the trees and stuff? Okay!'' He took a giant bite of his burger as if to signal his approval.

It was on Marc and Jason's favorite run—Porcupine on the resort's map, or Porkypine as Jason said it—that Heather had trouble. Afterwards she knew it was at least partly her own fault. She was racing. She had to admit it. And with a nine-year-old boy, to make matters worse. She got the jump on both Jason and Marc for the first time that afternoon just as a joke, pushing off down the slope while they were still adjusting their goggles. Jason turned to his dad, and they grinned at each other as they set off after her. Marc saw the whole thing happen right in front of him. Heather was skiing beautifully, but faster than she had on their earlier runs. She had gotten a quick lead and didn't want to lose it. That was when he saw another skier flash by, catch up with her, and cut in front on one of the gentle turns. She tried to dodge to her right but appeared to cross one ski tip over the other and went down in a cloud of snow. He was almost certain she had done a flip in the air.

Both father and son sprayed great curtains of snow as they slid to a stop beside her. Marc was relieved to see that both of her skis had come off as they were supposed to do. One was next to her, though the other had slid on its own some twenty feet away off the run into a low pine. But his momentary relief about her skis was brief. A sick feeling swept over him when he realized she was unconscious, and then he saw her right leg bent under her in an awkward position.

He snapped off his skis and jammed them crisscross fashion in the snow just above to signal that a skier was down. He dropped to his knees beside her and then turned to his son. ''Jason, she's going to need help. Can you ski to the bottom and get the ski patrol?''

Jason's eyes were wide with fear. ''Yes, Dad. She's not movin' or anything. Is she all right?''

''I hope so.'' Suddenly Heather groaned and her eyes flickered open, both welcome signs to father and son. "Now go. You know where the ski patrol is, don't you?"

"Yes."

"And be sure to tell them we're on Porcupine, about halfway down. Got that?" The boy nodded. "Be careful now."

"Yes, Dad." The words echoed back as Jason pushed off with his poles.

"Everything's going to be just fine," Marc said in a soothing voice. "The ski patrol will be here in a minute."

Heather's eyes opened again, and this time she tried with all her being to concentrate on the voice. It sounded hollow and otherworldly, like a tape played at slow speed. She closed her eyes and tried so hard to remember what had happened. She had started from the top. Yes. She was skiing too fast. She was flying down the slope, trying to keep her turns as tight as possible. But why? She wanted to stay ahead of someone. That was it. But then she heard the soft scratching sound of skis against snow as another skier overtook her on her left. She had to stay ahead. A figure crossed her path. She tried to turn. Or did she try to stop? She wasn't sure. The rest was a blur of trees and snow and skis and then darkness.

There was that voice again. So pleasant, so deep, so soothing. She struggled to make her eyes see where the voice was coming from. She focused on a pair of dark eyes locked on her. *Why, it's Marc Adams,* she realized in a flood of recognition. *He has the most beautiful eyes,* she decided suddenly, an observation that even to her seemed out of place. But the truly odd thing was that she didn't care. Those eyes mattered more than anything in the world at the moment. *Why does he look so worried?* she wondered. She strained to hear what he was saying, to make sense of those hollow-sounding words that she knew were coming from his mouth.

"Heather, are you all right? Can you hear me?"

"Yes. My leg." She groaned. She tried to move her right leg, which felt pinned beneath her.

"Don't move. You're going to be just fine. Help will be here any minute."

She tried to lift her shoulders, to sit up. She felt a panic at not being able to move her leg, and her eyes suddenly showed it. "I can't move. My leg."

Marc gently touched her shoulder. "Just stay quiet now." He took the glove off his right hand and caressed her forehead. He reached for her right hand, slipped off her heavy glove, and held her hand in his. The touch of his hand seemed to soothe her, and she lay back more comfortably. He thought about moving her leg—it looked so awkward—but decided against it. *Better to let those who know what they're doing take care of things,* he thought.

Heather licked her lips. "What happened?" she asked, and the look on her face was a little more coherent.

"You had an accident. Do you remember?"

She smiled suddenly. "Did I beat Jason?"

Marc felt a strange lightness, as if a weight had been lifted from his chest. She was going to be all right. He knew it now. When he first saw her there in the snow so motionless, he thought . . . well, he thought of that other time, the hospital, his emptiness. His body suddenly began to shake as he knelt by her side.

"Are you cold?" she asked, and her hand gripped his more firmly.

The next moments were a blur. Two members of the ski patrol swept down from the aid station at the top of the run. They were towing a yellow sled-stretcher, which they maneuvered next to Heather. They checked her quickly and expertly, first her eyes for pupil dilation, then her back and her legs and her arms for broken bones. Next they eased her right leg from its awkward position. She groaned in pain and squeezed Marc's hand hard as they straightened the leg. The medics next inflated a balloon splint over the knee to immobilize it and eased her carefully onto the sled. They snugged wide straps around her to keep her in place. Marc marveled at their efficiency. "Are you ready to travel, ma'am?" one of them asked with a smile. She nodded, let go of Marc's hand, and put both of her hands under the red wool blanket they had drawn up around her. One of the men had recovered her skis and poles, and these he secured on the sled. Then without another word they whisked her off down the slope.

Marc stood for a moment watching the sled disappear down

the mountain. Then he fastened his skis and finished the run, though much slower now. Jason was waiting at the bottom.

"Is she going to be all right, Dad?" he asked, his face somber.

"I think so, Jace. She was looking better by the time the patrol got there. Nice job going for help."

"I skied as fast as I could," the boy replied with such intensity that Marc put his arm around him and hugged him tight.

"I know you did. That's why the ski patrol got there so fast." Actually those minutes had seemed some of the longest of his life, but he didn't want the boy to know. "Now, let's get our skis off and see how she's doing."

They put their skis and poles in one of the racks by the front door of the lodge and hurried toward the infirmary.

"Mr. Adams!" a voice called suddenly.

Marc spun around toward the stopping area of the ski run. Shirley and Erik had just come down the slope. They poled toward him. "Have you seen Heather? I can't find her anywhere."

Shirley's face registered her growing concern as Marc related what had just happened. "Is she all right?"

"I think so. She was knocked out for a minute or so, but she was talking all right when the ski patrol took her away. She may have hurt her knee, though."

Shirley turned to Erik. "Did you hear that?"

He nodded. "Take off your skis and go with Mr. Adams to the aid station. I'll stow our things and meet you there." As Shirley, Marc, and Jason made their way toward the infirmary, Erik shouted after them, "They are very good here. The best I have ever seen. She will be fine."

There were two examining tables in the small first-aid station, each partitioned by movable curtains from a waiting area. Heather was sitting up on one of these tables as the three entered. The splint was gone from her knee and a large ice bag had replaced it. A doctor was hovering over her, peering into each of her eyes with a tiny flashlight, and a nurse was putting away a blood pressure cuff. The doctor straightened as they came in. "Are these the folks who were with you?"

"Yes, Mr. Adams and his son were," she answered.

The man directed his attention to Marc. "Did she lose consciousness at any time?"

"Yes, yes, she did."

"Would you have any idea how long? Thirty seconds? A minute? Five minutes?"

Marc scratched his head, recalling those frightening first moments when he wasn't certain how badly she had been injured. "I don't know for sure. Definitely not five minutes. Maybe a minute, but I don't think much longer than that. Everything seemed to be in slow motion."

The man turned back to Heather. "Are you experiencing a headache right now?"

"Yes," she answered truthfully, "a dull one."

"Blurred vision?"

"No, definitely not."

"Any nausea?"

"No."

"Follow this light." He moved his tiny flashlight in front of her face from one side to the other. She followed the beam dutifully. "Umm."

Shirley was growing weary of this medical business. "Is she all right?"

He turned and studied her with a smile. "I think she's going to be just fine." He turned back to Heather. "You may have suffered a mild concussion, but it shouldn't cause any problem. Now, as for the knee. I think it's a bad strain, but I want you to go to emergency down in Keats for an X ray. We don't have that kind of equipment here. You may have some ligament damage, but you've got pretty good range of motion. You didn't drive up here today, did you?"

"No," Shirley chimed in. "She came with me."

"Good. I want you to take her to the hospital right now. I'll call ahead so they'll be expecting you. Now, if you have any blurred vision, severe headache, nausea later tonight, call your doctor. Right?" Heather nodded. "Can you handle a pair of crutches?"

She grimaced. "I guess so. I've never tried."

Heather looked away from the television screen. She was watching an old James Stewart movie, or rather, she was *trying* to watch the movie. It was hard to concentrate with Shirley's constant interruptions. She worked her head in a slow arc very carefully, trying not to attract Shirley's attention. Her roommate had been playing nurse ever since they arrived home, and Heather was tiring of her attention, no matter how well-meaning. She grimaced as she stretched her shoulders. Her neck was stiff, and she still had a dull headache. She knew her body would be one big ache in the morning with the fall she'd taken. But at that she was lucky, and she knew it. Her leg was elevated on a kitchen chair cushioned by a pillow, a large ice bag snugged over the top of her knee. The hospital examination had shown no breaks and no tears. The doctor at Bear Claw had been right on the money with his diagnosis of a bad strain. Out of the corner of her eye she saw Shirley look toward her. *Uh-oh,* she said to herself, and feigned sudden interest in the movie.

"Are you okay?"

"Yes, I'm fine."

"You're not sick to your stomach, are you?"

"No."

"Have you got a headache?"

"I've got the same one I had five minutes ago when you asked me." Heather was losing her battle to keep the irritation out of her voice. She just didn't like people fussing over her. She never had.

"It isn't any worse, is it?"

"No, it isn't any worse."

"Can I get you anything? Something to drink? A little popcorn?"

"No, nothing."

Shirley leaned forward, concern etched on her face. "Are you sure you're not sick to your stomach?"

"Shirley! How can I watch a movie with you yammering every five seconds? No, I guarantee you I'm not sick to my stomach."

"I'm just following doctor's orders. How about your eyes? Is your vision blurry?"

Heather let out an exasperated sigh and stared at her roommate. "If you must know, I'm seeing two of everything on the television screen."

Shirley jumped to her feet. "Oh, my gosh, I'd better call Dr. Williams."

"Shirley, would you calm down? That's the way channel seven always looks. See for yourself. Ghosts."

Shirley stared at the screen. "Oh," she replied weakly and sat back down on the sofa. The doctor had told her not to let Heather go to sleep for at least six hours, and she was taking the assignment very seriously. Not willing to trust the TV to keep her roommate awake, she was relying on a steady barrage of conversation. "It was nice of Mr. Adams and Jason to come to the hospital, wasn't it?"

Heather looked at Shirley, but this time she smiled. "Yes," she said a little wistfully. Here was one distracting thought she didn't mind dwelling on. In fact, thinking back on the afternoon's frightening ordeal was not quite so unpleasant when she remembered Marc through it all. And Jason, for that matter. Marc had told her how the little guy had skied at breakneck speed to the bottom for help. But she remembered Marc's eyes most of all. The looks of panic and concern and then relief registering in turn in those dark eyes. *No, he obviously must not be a good poker player,* she thought. *He couldn't bluff his way out of a paper bag.* She leaned back against the cushion. She could almost feel the touch of his hand on her forehead and the comfort of his hand holding hers up there on the mountainside.

Shirley was standing close, waving her hand in front of Heather's face. "Are you all right? Are you awake?"

Heather broke from her reverie to stare at her roommate. "Shirley! Can't a girl have a little fantasy without you going totally crazy? I'm fine."

Shirley smiled with relief. "Well, how was I to know? You looked like you were in lala land."

"Well, maybe I was. Is there a law against that?"

Chapter Fifteen

Marc stood at the kitchen counter staring, unseeing, at the mountains outside the window. He hadn't slept well. In fact, he was positive he'd heard the big clock downstairs chime every hour through the night. It was the doctor's last-minute advice to Heather's roommate that sealed his sleepless night. "Don't let her sleep for six hours or so," he had said. That advice conjured up all kinds of dire consequences in Marc's mind and did nothing to ease the confusion in his head. For one thing he hadn't been able to account for the total emptiness he'd felt when he knelt by her as she lay unconscious in the snow. He argued with himself that it was only natural to be worried about someone's injury, especially someone you were skiing with. But he knew he was only deceiving himself. It was more than worry he had been feeling. But after all, she was his son's teacher. *Oh, right!* He hadn't shown such interest in his son's teachers the last couple of years.

He shook his head and slid open the cabinet drawer for the telephone directory. He paged through, searching for DeLaney, when it hit him. *She's new around here. She won't be in the book.* He stared at the ceiling, trying to remember the name of Heather's roommate. *It's Shirley something,* he said to himself. He walked down the hall to the studio. Jason was on the computer. "Hey, Jace, what's the name of Miss DeLaney's roommate? You know, the one we met yesterday? She's a first-grade teacher at your school."

Jason's eyes never left the monitor. "Miss Merrill. Why?"

"I want to call and see how Miss DeLaney is today."

"Okay, Dad."

Marc went back to the kitchen, found Shirley's name in the book, and punched in the numbers before he had time to talk himself out of it. He drummed his fingers on the counter as the phone rang. "Hello. Miss Merrill? This is Marc Adams. I was just wondering how Heather is getting along."

"That's good."

"I don't want to bother her. But sure, if she's up to it." He nervously switched the receiver to the other ear as Shirley stretched the phone to her roommate.

"Hello. How are you feeling?"

"I'm not surprised. You did a flip right over on your neck. How about the knee?"

"Well, remember, the doctor said to stay off of it as much as possible. You're not going to try to go to school tomorrow now, are you?"

"Are you sure that's a good idea? That's what sick days are for, you know."

"Come on! They ought to be able to get along for one or two days without you."

"Well, I guess you know best."

"I didn't really do anything. The ski patrol deserves all the credit."

"Didn't they do a good job? And the doctor at the aid station knew what he was doing too."

"Well, I'd better let you go. You need to rest. Sorry to bother you, but I promised Jason I'd call to see if there's going to be a sub tomorrow."

"No, he didn't really say that. I was just kidding!"

"Don't tell me you didn't love subs when you were in school."

"Sorry I reminded you. Now you'll go to school no matter what."

"Okay. 'Bye now." He hung up the phone slowly.

"How is Miss DeLaney feeling?"

Marc turned. Jason had just come into the kitchen with Smoky at his heels. "I didn't hear you, buddy. Oh, she seems a lot better today."

"That's good. What did you say about me?"

Marc was hoping Jason hadn't heard his little joke. "Oh, nothing much."

"I heard you say something," the boy persisted.

Marc knew he was caught. "I just kidded her that you wanted to know if there was going to be a sub tomorrow."

"Dad! I didn't say that."

"I know you didn't. I told her I was just kidding. Anyway, she's going to be at school."

"Good. Who you callin' now?"

Marc had been paging through the phone book again as the two were talking. "I thought I'd get her some flowers. Wouldn't that be nice?"

Jason was in the refrigerator rummaging for the juice container. "Uh-huh."

Marc found the name he was looking for, a woman who owned a florist shop just down the block from his gallery. He made the call and watched Jason pour a glass of orange juice as the phone rang. "Hello, Karen, this is Marc Adams."

"I'm fine. And you?"

"Good. Say, the shop's not open today, is it?"

"I didn't think so. I've got a big favor. Would it be possible to get a nice arrangement today?"

"I know it's a big imposition, but Jason's teacher had a skiing accident, and I thought I'd get something for her."

He smiled at Jason, who was watching his dad with a questioning look. "No, it's nothing like that. He's getting along just fine this year, but she's been really helpful."

"Dad!" the boy blurted.

Marc waved a hand at him. "Right. We just thought we'd drop it off this afternoon."

"One o'clock would be perfect."

"Karen, I really appreciate this. I owe you big time. See you about one." He hung up the phone.

"Dad, you made me sound like a big brownnoser."

"I don't think I made you sound that way. Anyway, you want to get something nice for Miss DeLaney, don't you?"

"Well, yes," the boy said dubiously.

"So that's exactly what we're going to do."

* * *

The doorbell rang. Heather was sitting awkwardly at the kitchen table, her right leg propped on a chair. She was correcting a set of spelling papers. Shirley was at the other end of the table, mounting cutout vowels on colorful construction paper. They were both keeping an eye on the Broncos game on the TV in the living room. "Now who could that be?" Shirley asked as she threw Heather a questioning glance. Heather shrugged her shoulders and began to reach for the crutches leaning against the table. "No, you sit still," Shirley said. "I'll get it." She sprang off her chair and headed for the door.

"You're going to spoil me if you keep this up."

Shirley didn't hear the last remark; she was already opening the door. "Hello, Mr. Adams. Come in."

Heather looked down at herself. She was wearing a pair of dark green sweatpants and a tattered white University of Colorado sweatshirt. She grimaced at the thought of how she must look, but all she had time to do to improve her appearance was to fluff her hair just as Marc came around the corner carrying what was obviously a large arrangement of flowers. She could see the pink and green of the flowers and foliage through the plastic wrap protecting the delicate blossoms from the cold outside.

"Well, hello. This is a surprise," she managed.

He was holding the flower arrangement awkwardly in front of him. "Jason and I thought some flowers might make you feel a little better."

She was clearing a space in front of her on the table. "Put them right here so I can look at them." He gladly set the vase down where she pointed and stepped back. She undid the wrapping carefully, revealing a delicate arrangement of pink roses, white daisies, and darker pink carnations with baby's breath in a robin's egg blue ceramic vase. "They're beautiful. Shirley, look. Aren't they lovely? It reminds me of spring, and we haven't even gotten to winter yet."

"And look at the vase," Shirley added. "Doesn't it have the prettiest shape?"

Marc was standing with his hands draped over the back of one of the chairs, trying not to look too pleased with himself.

Heather looked up at him and smiled. "You didn't have to do this."

"It's the least we could do. After all, we were kind of a part of your accident. If you hadn't met up with us, it probably never would have happened."

"I doubt that. If it was going to happen, it was going to happen." She adjusted several of the flowers to better advantage and raised an eyebrow as she looked at him. "But come to think of it, I *was* racing both of you down the slope. And you hadn't been playing fair all afternoon." She corrected herself when she saw Marc was ready to object. "Well, at least Jason hadn't been. He kept getting a big head start."

"I think it only right," Shirley said in mock seriousness, "in the interest of Jason, who isn't here to defend himself, that I remind you he is only nine years old and deserves a head start."

"Did you see him ski?" Heather demanded. "He's good." A questioning look suddenly crossed her face. "Where is he, anyway?"

"He's in the car."

"Well, have him come in. He'll get cold out there."

"He'll be fine. I'm only going to stay a minute," Marc insisted. "Besides, he's up to his eyeballs in some video game."

"He likes his video games, doesn't he?" Heather said with a laugh.

Marc smiled and tapped his fingers nervously on the back of the chair. He glanced toward Shirley. There was an awkward silence. Shirley fought back a smile and succeeded in keeping it from registering everywhere but her eyes. They narrowed ever so slightly in mirth. *You don't need to knock old Shirley in the head,* she thought. *I know when it's time to make myself scarce.* "Say, why don't I put the flowers on the coffee table?"

Heather slipped a finger inside the vase. "They've got plenty of water." Shirley scooped up the vase and hurried to the living room with it.

"They'll be perfect right here," she said as she positioned the vase on the oak table. "Now if you two will excuse me, I've got to put a call in to Erik. He told me to check in with him this afternoon."

Heather watched her roommate scurry down the hall to her room. She was positive Shirley had told her it was impossible to call Erik when he was out on the slopes.

As he surveyed the flower arrangement in its new location, Marc spotted the TV. "Any score in the game?"

Heather glanced toward the screen. "Just before you got here the Broncos fumbled the ball away, and they were already down ten–zip," she said, disgusted. "I think that's where it still stands. I thought this was going to be their year, but I've just about given up."

"No, things don't look promising, that's for sure," he said as he did his finger exercises on the back of the chair again. The two watched the screen in silence for several moments.

"Why don't you sit down?"

"No, I'm fine. I've got to be going anyway." He cleared his throat. "I was wondering," he began hesitantly, "would you like to have dinner Friday night?"

Heather looked back from the TV toward him. She was only partly successful at keeping her surprise from showing. "You mean hot dogs and potato chips?" she asked with a laugh.

The laugh was good medicine for the tension he was feeling inside. He smiled, suddenly more at ease. "I was thinking of a little more than that. Just the two of us."

"Sounds great."

"Good. I'll pick you up, say about seven. All right?"

"That's perfect."

It had been years since he had asked a woman out, and he was definitely out of practice. The thought had been spinning around in the recesses of his brain for some time now—actually, he decided, since that conference at school he had handled so badly. But heaven knew, he might never have gotten up enough courage to act on that thought if it hadn't been for Jason's little "dinner party." She was so perfect in the way she handled Jason's strange menu. And she was so easy to talk to. So interested and interesting. He knew then that he had to get to know her better. And the accident yesterday only confirmed it. He had to find out the meaning of what he had felt up there on the mountain. Right now he was like some silly high school kid who had landed a weekend date with a cheerleader. But he was thirty-two years old, he reminded himself, known for nothing if not his reserved manner. He was feeling anything but reserved at this moment, and he knew he'd better get out before he said something really stupid.

"Well, I'd better be going." He started to back toward the door. "Jason's waiting. You take it easy now. Stay off that knee as much as possible."

"Yes, Doctor," she joked. "Thanks again for the flowers. They're beautiful. And tell Jason thanks."

"Okay," he said as he backed into a chair by the front door. "Whoops." He realigned the chair, turned quickly, and fumbled with the door. " 'Bye," he called as he let himself out.

"Bye-bye," Heather called after him. She had to stifle a giggle at his antics.

Shirley had been sitting quietly on her bed with the door closed, waiting for Marc to leave. Unable to hear what was going on between the two, she was dying of curiosity. When she heard the front door slam, she dashed out to the kitchen, ready for the lowdown. "What was that all about?"

"Oh, nothing much."

"Come on. He was as nervous as a turtle on the freeway."

Heather laughed. "He was, wasn't he? He just invited me to dinner."

"You're kidding. Not hot dogs and baked beans again?"

"No, we're going out. Just the two of us," Heather said with a smug look for her roommate.

"Well, la di da, Miss Smarty. And all you had to do was throw yourself down a mountain."

"Don't remind me," Heather said as she checked the ice bag resting on her knee.

Jason stuck his video game into the car's center console as Marc climbed in. "Did she like the flowers?"

"I think so. She acted like it, anyway."

The boy suddenly gave his dad an inquisitive squint. "How come you're lookin' so dopey?"

Marc started the car and glanced over at his son. "What's that supposed to mean?"

"You've got a dopey grin on your face."

Marc leaned forward in the seat and studied himself in the rearview mirror. He did have a kind of lopsided grin pasted on his face, he decided, and the more he tried to get rid of it, the more it widened.

"See. You do have a dopey grin, don't ya?"

Marc reached over and poked his son lightly in the ribs. "I guess I'm just in a good mood. You got a problem with that, buddy?"

"Nope. I like it when you're in a good mood. 'Cuz then sometimes we go out for pizza."

Marc chuckled as he slipped the car into gear and pulled away from the curb. "You're a real con artist, you know it?"

"What's a con artist?"

"Never mind. You're just one, that's all."

Jason leaned back against the seat and stretched his arms back over the headrest. "Dad?"

"What, big guy?"

"I sure like Miss DeLaney. Don't you?"

Marc shot a surprised look at his son. "Yes, I do," he volunteered. He turned back to the road in front of him. "I really do," he said more quietly.

Chapter Sixteen

Heather barely survived Monday at school. It was almost a repeat of her posthaircut day. The kids were full of questions the second they walked through the door and saw a crutch leaning against her desk. At least by Monday morning she was down to one crutch, and she might have sneaked away to school without even that if it hadn't been for her chief nurse, Shirley. And the fact that the two were carpooling made any sneaking completely out of the question. Deep down she knew her roommate was right. The knee was still sore and swollen slightly, and it would be foolhardy to put her full weight on it just yet. She wasn't about to admit that to Shirley, though.

Answering a zillion questions about her accident was only part of the problem. She found herself nearly rooted to her desk for the day. And for a teacher like Heather, always on the move wandering through the classroom checking on the kids and watching their work, such immobility was much more than just a nuisance. She felt less effective as a teacher, even though most of the kids were practically coming out of their skins trying to help her, volunteering for anything and everything.

Jason proved to be a real irritation. He was enjoying his eye-witness status just a little too much to suit her. When she tried to describe the accident to the class right after the bell rang so she could get the whole business out of the way, he kept interrupting with more detail, intending to let everyone know he was there when the accident happened. "You were skiing too fast, weren't you, Miss DeLaney?" he butted in with right at the beginning. "Don't forget to tell them you were knocked out," he blurted at another point in her story. "She got to ride in one of

117

those ambulance sleds,'' he came up with next. She gave him her mildly withering look, but it sailed right over his head. No doubt about it, he was not the same painfully shy boy who had walked into her classroom the first day of school. She was happy for the change certainly, but she wouldn't have minded having the old quiet Jason back just for this one day. Heather watched as the kids turned toward him, hanging on his words, and she had to admit with a hint of a smile that she couldn't for the world blame him.

She stood at the door, leaning on her one crutch at the end of the day, saying good-bye to the kids as they left. Next she made her way back to her desk and collapsed into the chair. She was exhausted. She pulled the stack of geography tests toward her, took out her red pencil, and set to work. She was midway through the third test when a sharp rap on the door frame brought her head up with a jerk. Miss Nordway was standing at the door, looking surprisingly crisp for the end of the day in a neatly tailored dark brown suit. She stepped in and strolled slowly toward Heather's desk, looking about the room as she always did.

Heather had learned from Shirley that the teachers hated having the woman anywhere near their rooms. They found her critical eye intrusive. Many reported receiving notes in their mailboxes after a Nordway walkthrough about the most trivial things. Shirley claimed that she personally saw one note that chided a teacher because the window blinds were not lined up evenly at the bottom. Knowing Shirley, Heather decided that story could be a joke, but she wasn't sure. She had to admit the principal made her uneasy, though to date she hadn't received one of the infamous notes. Heather studied Miss Nordway closely as she came nearer. She was trying to fathom the look the woman had on her face. It was as if a sympathetic mask she had dropped into place before entering the room was battling with the hint of an amused smile. The smile was bothersome.

''I heard about your accident. I'm so sorry,'' she said with more than a trace of theatrical emotion in her voice. *Gushing* was the word Shirley used to describe Miss Nordway's approach, and Heather had to admit it was a pretty good word. Heather had discovered at the onset of her teaching career that elementary teachers, especially those in the primary grades, often talked to children in that way. In fact, she thought she did it sometimes herself, and she knew Shirley did too. *If you stay at it too long,* she had wondered more than once, *do you start to talk to everyone that way?*

"It was nothing. Just a strained knee."

"That isn't what I heard. It could have been very serious for you." She punctuated her words with a wag of her finger. Heather could see the long fingernail painted a bright crimson.

Where did she get that information? Heather wondered. *Has Jason been giving interviews?* "I was knocked out for a few seconds, and that was a little scary. But aside from that, everything they did was basically precautionary."

"You can never be too careful with a head injury." There went the finger again. "You want to be very careful of headaches. You aren't having any, are you?"

Aha! It is *Shirley,* Heather thought. *She's been talking to Shirley.* "I had a pretty bad one right after it happened, but I've been feeling fine since then."

"Well, don't take any chances with a head injury. Headache, blurred vision, nausea. If you experience any of those, you call your doctor."

This is one of Shirley's little jokes. I'm going to get her if it's the last thing I do.

"Yes, the doctor warned me, but I've been feeling fine. Except I have to stay off the knee for a few days." She nodded at the crutch.

"Yes, I meant to talk to you at lunch about that, but I had a sudden emergency in my office. Why don't you take a few days off lunchroom duty? It must be so hard hobbling about on that thing," she said, the sympathy fairly dripping.

Heather had no intention of taking Miss Nordway up on the offer. The last thing she would ever be accused of was shirking her duty. "Oh, it's not that bad. I'm getting quite good at it, to tell the truth."

"Well, whatever you think best. But you follow your doctor's orders." Heather expected the shaking of the finger on that one, but it didn't happen. "How fortunate our friend Mr. Adams happened along when he did."

Heather was so surprised at this remark she was certain it

showed. It wasn't so much what the principal said as how she said it. Certainly she could have heard about Marc's part in her rescue any number of ways. Maybe she overheard Jason's account of the accident during lunch or after school. Maybe Shirley mentioned it, but Heather doubted that. She watched Miss Nordway's face closely. The hint of a smile she'd noticed when the woman came in was now obvious. *Did she come in here to confirm a suspicion that I was skiing with Marc? What if I was? What's the big deal anyway? There's no rule against going skiing with a parent, is there? Of course, maybe there is in Miss Nordway's book of rules,* she thought. *I wasn't skiing with him, anyway. I just happened to see him there with Jason. And, after all, Jason is one of my students.*

All these thoughts flashed through her mind at lightning speed before she spoke. "He was very helpful" was all she could come up with.

"And isn't it all very odd," Miss Nordway went on, "that the very man who tried so hard to keep the district from hiring you is the one who ends up saving your life practically. Isn't life just full of strange irony?"

While Heather was trying to figure out how to answer that one, Miss Nordway was off again. "But as I remember he's been quite helpful around school this year. Didn't he go along on one of your field trips?"

"Yes, he did." *You know darned well he did,* she was thinking.

"You can't imagine what a turnaround there's been in that man. I don't know if you've heard the stories, but last year I dreaded seeing him walk in the building. What a change! How strange, but pleasantly so, wouldn't you say?"

"Definitely," Heather agreed. Her knowledge of the old Marc was certainly limited, but it was personal. In spite of the good things that had happened between them, she hadn't forgotten how he acted on their first meeting. If that was typical of the Marc Adams of the last couple of years, then, yes, just about anything could be considered an improvement.

"But you've done wonders with that boy of his."

Heather squirmed uncomfortably. "I really haven't done all that much."

"Oh, but you have. And his father can thank his lucky stars

we didn't let him bully us about hiring you.'' She waved a hand at Heather. ''Now don't be so modest.'' She turned abruptly on her heel. ''I'm keeping you from your work. And I have a four o'clock conference myself.'' Her tone became confidential. ''We had a little trouble this morning just outside the front door before school. Maybe you heard. Third graders. Can you imagine? I don't know what the world is coming to when little third graders fight like common thugs. You take care of yourself now.'' She headed for the door with her quick little steps. She stopped once and picked a small piece of paper from the floor and deposited it in the wastebasket by the door. Then she was gone.

Heather let out a deep sigh and rolled her eyes at the ceiling. *What is it with her? She was pouring on the sugar, but I still have a funny feeling she was up to no good.* She looked back at the test she was correcting and tried to remember where she'd left off.

''Hey, don't look at me,'' Shirley insisted. Heather and Shirley were on their way home, and Heather had just hinted that her roommate might have blabbed to the principal. ''I didn't talk to Miss Myway once today, and that's just the way I like it.''

''Then how did she find out about Marc coming to my rescue Saturday?''

Shirley was driving, and she shot Heather a quick glance. ''Spies.''

''Spies?''

''Oh, sure, she has spies everywhere. She's got a better spy network than the CIA.''

''Oh, come on.''

''Well, maybe I'm exaggerating. Her network probably isn't better than the CIA.'s, but at least it's just as good.'' She looked over at Heather. ''Seriously, I don't know how she finds out things; I just know she does.''

''She sure doesn't seem to care much for Marc.''

Shirley pulled to a stop at a red light. ''Can you blame her? I have a feeling he made things a little uncomfortable around here the last couple of years. Since his wife and daughter died, really.''

''So I gathered.''

The light changed, and Shirley made her turn off Highway 17

onto Rayburn Road. "But that's all changed now since you tamed him." She turned with a grin. "Right?"

"I'm telling you, we're just friends. I've had some success with his boy, and he appreciates it."

"That was all true in phase one. But now you're moving on to phase two—the date. Not that there's anything wrong with that, mind you. He's eligible. I should say he's eligible." She took one hand off the wheel and tallied with her fingers. "Let's see, he's good-looking. He's a famous artist. He has a nice son he obviously adores. He lives in a beautiful house. He's probably fabulously wealthy. Hey, what more could a girl ask for?"

Heather looked at her roommate, a slight smile betraying her feelings. "Shirley!"

But Shirley wasn't through yet. "Not that there aren't problems on the horizon. He's got some bad memories he's carrying around in that handsome head of his that would be tough for any man to deal with. It's obvious he's been floundering the last couple of years. So Aunt Shirley's just giving you fair warning. It's not going to be all smooth sailing."

Heather shook her head. "Honestly, you sound just like my mother. Any man I ever go out with, she's always sizing him up for a wedding tux. Have you ever heard of just being friends?"

"Of course, that's how most relationships start. You don't marry an enemy." She laughed. "On second thought, I guess some people do. But they don't do it on purpose unless there's something wrong with their heads."

The two fell silent. Heather stared out the window at the mountains in the waning sunlight. Their white blanket was beginning to thicken as fall moved to winter, at least at the high elevations. She couldn't help thinking about what Shirley had said. Were she and Marc moving to another phase, as "Aunt" Shirley was hinting? She liked him; there was no question about that. He could be so kind and tender. She thought again about the touch of his hand as she lay on the ski slope last Saturday. *And he is so good with Jason. Shirley's right about that. He really does adore the boy. That's why he caused so much trouble at school the last two years—he was obviously worried to death about him.*

She sighed so loudly that Shirley glanced over at her. *There's such a strength about the man,* she thought, *but at the same time he's so sensitive too. I guess that must be the artist in him. He doesn't see things like everyone else.* Strangely now she remembered the loathing she had felt for him at her job interview, when he stomped by her in the hall on his way out of the building. *How could my feelings for him change so completely?* Her answer came in the form of a favorite saying of her mother's: hate is the closest thing to love. Those words had meant nothing to her before, but now . . . now she wasn't so sure.

"Good morning, sunshine." Heather looked about her with a start. They were sitting in front of the condo, and Shirley was grinning at her. "Penny for your thoughts."

Heather smiled sheepishly. "It's all your fault, Aunt Shirley. You and all of this business about phase two."

Shirley climbed out of the car and reached in the back for her oversize bag and Heather's briefcase and crutch. She stopped suddenly and grinned at her roommate over the front seat. "All I was trying to do was keep you aware of your possibilities, and look at the thanks I get."

Heather pushed herself up from the dinner table and began to clear the dishes. Shirley jumped up. "Here, let me do that. You need to be careful of that knee."

"Shirley, stop pampering me. You're going to turn me into a vegetable. You've been doing everything for me since Saturday. Now sit down in the living room, put your feet up, and read the paper. I can handle this."

"Are you sure?"

"Yes, I'm positive."

Reluctantly, Shirley turned the kitchen over to her roommate and retreated, grumbling, to the living room. At first, Heather tried carrying dishes to the sink with one hand while she maneuvered the crutch with the other. Before long, she abandoned the crutch altogether in favor of hopping on one leg. She found she could make it from the table to the counter in three short hops.

"What's going on out there?"

"Nothing. I'm just hopping."

"Well, you sound like an oversize kangaroo," Shirley called as the doorbell rang. "Now who could that be? Stay where you are; I'll get it."

Heather was just putting the last dishes in the dishwasher when she heard the familiar voice at the door. *Jess.* She hadn't seen her cousin in ages. *Wonder what she wants?* she thought. She grabbed her crutch and made her way to the living room.

"There you are!" Jess exclaimed. "I've been trying to reach you for hours. Do you two spend all your time on the phone?"

Heather and Shirley glanced questioningly at each other. "We haven't touched the phone since we got home, have we?" Heather asked.

"Nope, we haven't touched it," Shirley agreed. She went straight to the wall phone in the kitchen and lifted the receiver. "Nothing but static," she said with a frown. "No dial tone at all." She grinned at Heather. "Why, who knows how many valuable calls we've missed?"

"Well, I know one you missed," Jess insisted. She was standing in the living room, her hands on her hips, staring at Heather. "I was worried sick when I heard you were hobbling around school on crutches. What in the world happened?"

Heather dropped onto the sofa and gently lifted her injured leg onto the hassock. "How did you hear all that? Tim and Ellen saw me, I suppose."

"Those two!" Jess exclaimed. "I swear they wander around in a fog half the time. I had to hear about it from my next-door neighbor, Charlotte Ramsey. She volunteers in the library on Mondays. I don't think you've met her, but she knows we're cousins. Anyway, she saw you. When I asked the kids about you, they both acted like they'd been out in the sun too long. 'Oh, yeah, Mom, we forgot to tell you.' Duh! They forgot to tell me my cousin was hobbling around on crutches?"

Heather laughed. "That all sounds strangely familiar. Anyway, why should they worry about you? They know you already have your own devious methods for finding out about everything. Right?"

"Spy networks," Shirley said with a grin. "Didn't I tell you?"

"I'm beginning to think you may be right."

Jess unzipped her jacket and slipped into the recliner. "Don't bad-mouth our fine news-gathering system. We'd never make it through the boring winters around here without some juicy gossip." She waved her hands in front of her. "But I didn't come all the way across town to talk about that. I want to know what happened.''

Shirley raised her hand. ''Excuse me, ladies. I've heard this story a time or two, as I recall. If you don't mind, I'm going to slip next door to the McCormicks' to see if I can report our phone trouble.'' She caught Jess's eye with a raised eyebrow. ''Now no matter what she tells you, she was not practicing on the two-mile Olympic slalom run.''

As Shirley turned for the door, Heather caught her square in the back of the head with a small pillow. ''Take that for ruining my best story,'' Heather said, and she giggled as Shirley retrieved the pillow and hurled it back.

''You two are worse than my kids,'' Jess grumbled good-naturedly. ''At least I know you're not at death's door.'' She tried to glare. ''Not that you'd ever call a favorite cousin when you have an accident. No. I have to find out about it through my sources.''

''I didn't want to worry you, Jess. It was no big deal.'' Shirley had gone out the door by now, and Heather told the story of the skiing accident, leaving out none of the details.

Jess was a good listener. She grimaced at all the right places and even held her head at the thought of doing a complete flip on the hard snow. ''It's a wonder you weren't killed. Did you call your folks?''

''Are you kidding? Mom would probably be on the next plane. Anyway, Dad promised to drive out in the next couple of weeks for some skiing, and I thought I'd tell him then. Hopefully this silly knee will be better by then so I can go skiing with him.''

''And I understand our friend Marc Adams came to your rescue?''

Heather would have come clear off the sofa at that news if her leg hadn't been stretched out on the hassock. As it was, she felt a twinge of pain in the knee as she lurched forward. ''Where did you hear that?''

''My neighbor Charlotte,'' Jess said in surprise at her cousin's reaction. ''Why? Isn't it true?''

''Yes, it's true. It's just that Miss Nordway came calling after school with the same information. And somehow or other she ended up giving me a guilt trip about it.''

"Why in the world would you feel guilty about that?"

"Because I have his son in my class."

Jess had a perplexed look on her face. She sat for a moment while the latest information sank in. "Oh," she said finally. "I thought Marc Adams just happened along. I didn't know you were skiing with him. Not that there's anything wrong with that."

"I wasn't exactly skiing with him. I mean, I didn't go there with him. I met him and Jason there, and we skied for a while."

"So? There's no law against that, is there?"

"No, not that I know of. But the way Miss Nordway acted, I'm not so sure."

Jess waved a hand. "Oh, don't worry about her. She's a fuddy-duddy about everything. I swear she has the personality of a carp."

Heather laughed. "Jess, that's a horrible thing to say."

"Well, it's true. Haven't you noticed? She even looks like a carp. She always puckers her lips together like this." She pursed her lips like a goldfish kissing the side of its bowl. "Just like a carp."

Heather was giggling. "Stop it. Now every time I see her, all I'm going to think about is a carp."

"Well, it's the truth." Jess popped the footrest out on the recliner. "So, you and Marc Adams have got something going, huh?"

"No, I wouldn't say that."

"What does that mean? Are you dating him or not?"

Heather moved uncomfortably on the sofa. "Not really."

Jess glared. "Honestly, you are so stingy with details. Now what in the world does 'not really' mean?"

Heather's face reddened. "I did have dinner at his house last Friday."

Jess's eyes sparkled. "Now we're getting someplace. Tell me more."

"It's not what you think," Heather added. Then she filled her cousin in on the dinner, including the invitation and the three-hot-dog meal.

"Ah, isn't that sweet," Jess said in a baby voice. "The little guy likes his teacher."

Heather shot her cousin an angry look. "I thought it was cute. He planned it all himself."

Jess grinned at her cousin's flare of temper. "Don't bite my head off, little cousin. It must be a teacher thing, huh? I'm sorry. You're right; it was nice of him. But what about his dad? Doesn't he like the teacher a little bit too?"

"Well, we're going out to dinner this Friday, if you must know," Heather said with a defiant little toss of her head.

Jess raised an eyebrow as she studied her cousin. "Just the two of you?" Heather nodded. "Aha, that's more like it. Why didn't you tell me that in the first place?"

"It's no big deal."

" 'It's no big deal,' " Jess mimicked. "Here we go again with the denial stuff."

"You sound just like Shirley, and she sounds just like my mother. I'm telling you we're just friends."

"Okay, we'll let it go at that," said Jess with a smile that suggested she had no intention of doing anything of the sort. "You have to admit even *that's* something. I remember the afternoon you came home from your job interview. Wow! You were ready to slash his tires."

"I wasn't that bad."

"Just about. What a turnaround." Jess snapped the recliner footrest back and stood up. "I've got to run. I told Jerry I'd be right back once I found out you were in the land of the living." She zipped her jacket. "He's changed, you know."

"Who? Jerry?" Heather said with a smirk.

"No, Smarty, Marc Adams. My friend Doris . . . you know she works for him at the gallery . . . she says he's been a different person the last month or so. More like his old self. She says his painting's better too. He's turned out some stuff that looks like the old Marc Adams. According to her, he's a lot more talkative too." Jess gave Heather a sly smile. "You don't suppose love has come into his life?"

Heather's face reddened. "I wouldn't know."

"Uh-huh. Well, if you do find out, you'll let your cousin Jess in on it, won't you?"

"You'll be the first to know."

"I bet," she said sarcastically. "It's like pulling teeth to get anything out of you.'' She leaned over and gave Heather an affectionate pat on the shoulder. ''You take care of that knee, now, you hear? I've gotta run. Don't move. I can find my way out. If you ever get that phone fixed, use it once in a while, will you?''

''I will. I promise,'' Heather said. '' 'Bye. Thanks for coming.'' She watched as Jess headed for the door, then saw her do a quick detour toward the flowers, which had been moved from the coffee table to a bookshelf. Shirley had complained that she couldn't see the television with the flowers on the table.

''What have we here? Pretty flowers.'' She read the card, a simple *Sorry about your accident.* It was signed *Marc and Jason.* ''Well, the message is pretty lame, but you know what they say about flowers—the symbol of love.'' She turned to smile at her cousin just in time to catch a pillow aimed at her head. She wagged a finger and clicked her tongue. ''You're going to hurt someone, if you're not careful. What a way for a teacher to act. Now what could be causing such violent behavior? Could it be the bite of the lovebug?'' She threw the pillow back and streaked for the door. ''Bye-bye, little cousin,'' she called as she slipped out the door, and Heather could hear the giggle she loved.

''Good-bye and good riddance,'' Heather shouted with a laugh as she launched another pillow. This time it bounced harmlessly off the back of the door as it closed.

She leaned back against the sofa, trying to digest everything she had just heard. It was obvious Marc had changed. She knew that, but she thought it was just toward her because of her success with Jason. *Could it really be more than that?* she wondered.

Chapter Seventeen

Heather paced from the front window to the living room, wringing her hands. She was waiting for Marc, and every other minute she stopped at the window, slipped the curtain aside, and checked for his car. At least it was good to be able to walk on both legs for a change, she decided. She had gone to the doctor after school, and Dr. Williams had given the okay to throw away the one remaining crutch. The knee was feeling much better, and the doctor had outlined a series of exercises to make it even stronger. He said he thought Heather should be back on the slopes in two weeks' time.

"Would you please sit down?" Shirley said from the recliner. "You're going to be back on crutches again if you don't rest that leg. For heaven's sake, he'll get here when he gets here."

Heather sat on the edge of the sofa, but she was on her feet again, peering out the window, at the sound of a car driving past. She crouched to see herself in the oval mirror over the bookshelf where Marc's flowers, beginning to droop, waited to be tossed. She went to stand in front of Shirley. "Do I look all right?"

Shirley put aside her newspaper, cocked her head, and squinted knowingly as she appraised her roommate. Heather was wearing a long-sleeved, navy blue knit dress with a turtleneck collar. The dress showed off her trim figure nicely. Her only jewelry consisted of a simple silver chain and silver hoop earrings. "Considering you don't have the slightest idea where you're going, you look fine."

Heather glanced down at her shoes, doubt showing on her face. The shoes were a simple black pair with medium heels. "I don't

129

know about these shoes. Do you think the heels are high enough?''

''They're fine. They're middle-of-the-road. If you go to a fancy-schmancy place, they'll be great, or if you go dancing at Bruno's, they'll be okay too.''

Heather gave her roommate a withering look. ''We're not going to Bruno's.''

''Well, you never know. Just in case you do, you'll be all ready. Of course, the Bruno's crowd goes in for a bit more leather than you're showing. How come you didn't find out where you were going, anyway?''

Heather made a face. ''I was so shocked I didn't think to ask.'' She smiled when she thought of Marc's nervousness. ''Even if I had thought about it, I don't think I would have asked anyway.'' She noticed a pair of car headlights through the curtain and hurried again to the window. ''He's here.''

Shirley smiled from behind her newspaper. ''Calm down, would ya? You'd think you'd never been on a date before.''

Heather checked herself again in the mirror. ''I know. I don't know what's wrong with me.'' The doorbell rang, and she jumped at the sound. She looked frantically about her. ''Where's my purse? I thought I put it right here on the chair.''

''Aren't you going to let the poor man in?''

Heather went to the door, stood long enough to take a deep breath, and opened it. ''Hello,'' she said brightly, hoping she wasn't sounding too much like a fourth-grade teacher on the first day of school. ''Come in. I seem to have misplaced my purse. I'll only be a moment.'' She scurried toward her bedroom.

He stepped in and smiled at Shirley. She had put the newspaper aside and was watching him. *This is more entertaining than television,* she decided. She was glad Heather had dressed up when she checked him over. He was wearing dark brown slacks, a burgundy turtleneck, and a gorgeous sport coat that Shirley was positive had to be cashmere. ''Hello, Miss Merrill,'' he said.

''Oh, please, just Shirley. I'm only Miss Merrill during the week, thank goodness. Aren't you going to be cold without a coat?''

''I have one in the car, but it really doesn't feel half bad out. It's just starting to snow. Big flakes.''

"That will make Erik happy. I've never known anyone who liked snow as much as he does. If it's a wet snow, be careful of that beautiful jacket. You wouldn't want to get it wet."

He looked down at his coat. "Hm. I never thought of that. I'm too used to indestructible jeans and a sweatshirt. Thanks."

Just then Heather swept back into the room with a small clutch purse in hand. "I left it on the dresser. I swear I don't know if my head's fastened on."

Marc's eyes widened when she stopped long enough for him to get a good look at her. He had never seen her look so beautiful. Suddenly his mouth gaped in surprise. "I just noticed, no crutch. Is that on doctor's orders or are you cheating?"

"No, I got the okay this afternoon. And it feels so good not to have to worry about that stupid thing."

"Are we ready?" he asked as he turned toward the door.

"I think so, as soon as I get my coat." She grabbed her long black coat off the hanger and began to struggle into it. He stepped over quickly and held it for her. "Oh, thank you." She pulled open the door and stopped to smile back at Shirley. "See you later."

"Right. Have fun, you two." She watched them go out and then with the hint of a smile on her face she looked heavenward. "Take care of them. They're going to need it."

The two chatted easily on the way to the restaurant. They talked about Jason mainly, and Heather filled the father in on his son's latest exploits at school. It was easy to praise the boy. He was turning into one of her best students, and Marc never tired of hearing the good news after two years of quite the opposite. As they talked, she watched with fascination as giant flakes of snow struck the front window of the car, flattening into icy wafers before the wipers swept them away. She still had no idea where they were going, but then, it made no difference to her. People raved about the restaurants in the town of Keats, so a night out just about anywhere was bound to please.

Because of the tourist and skiing crowd, Keats boasted a selection of first-rate nightspots amazing for a town of its size. A noted Denver food critic had featured a sampling of its restaurants in a spread for the *Post* a couple of years back. In it he called

Keats "the poor man's Aspen." Townspeople were angered by what they thought was a slur when it first appeared in print until someone realized the commercial value of being compared to Colorado's glitziest tourist mecca. Then the quote was adopted as a slogan for the community and distributed widely on anything and everything about Keats as proof that good old Joshua Keats's little town had finally arrived. Heather had visited only a handful of eateries since moving here and had yet to sample the cuisine at a place worthy of the revered Denver food critic's notice, but as they pulled into the parking lot of Antonio's, she knew all that was about to change.

Antonio's was one of Keats's most respected nightspots. She even remembered the names of half a dozen well-known Hollywood stars who had been seen dining here just in the last couple of weeks. More and more celebrities from the worlds of sports, music, television, politics, and the movies now made their way to Keats as much for the pace of things as for the ideal skiing conditions. Keats moved at its own speed and wouldn't be hurried for anyone. And locals followed a strict unspoken rule—no stargazing, at least none that the star would feel uncomfortable with. Paparazzi found no welcome mat in this little mountain valley.

"Have you tried Antonio's?" Marc asked as he slipped the car into a space in the parking lot, which was not yet crowded at this relatively early dining hour.

Heather glanced at him. "No, I haven't."

"It's been a couple of years since I've been here myself. I hope the food is still as good as I remember."

The restaurant was unremarkable on the outside. It was, in the manner of many buildings in the area, constructed of wooden beams and rough timber with the aim, Heather supposed, of taking the visitor back to the early life of the town. She noted, as they stepped in the front door, that the "early silver mine" roughness was carried out inside as well. But the furnishings were impressive. Genuine antiques, from what Heather could tell. In the waiting area she saw a glass-front china closet filled with crystal of every description imaginable. A monstrous hand-carved grandfather clock rested at the entrance to the lounge to their right. She could see stained-glass windows, Tiffany lamps, a polished bar. The whole place was a feast for the eyes even in such subdued light.

She was still registering all these sights as a rotund, middle-aged man with a florid face and thinning hair slicked across a gleaming pate, approached to greet them. He was impeccably dressed in a dark suit, dazzlingly white shirt, and dark tie, and his manner was quite formal, though pleasant. He bowed slightly toward the pair. "Ah, Mr. Adams. How good to see you again. I have your favorite table waiting."

"Thank you, Antonio," Marc said, and Heather thought she heard a strained quality in his voice.

"May I take your wraps?" They shed their coats, which he passed on to a smiling young woman standing nearby. "Now, if you will follow me, please."

The two fell into step behind him as he led them into the restaurant itself. Heather was at first shocked at the small size of the dining area despite its high ceiling, until she realized the dining room was ringed with smaller, more intimate rooms. It was into one of these that Antonio led them. The room was cozy, with a gentle fire dancing in a stone fireplace on one wall. There were three tables separated at some distance, and Antonio placed them at one of these. He bowed again. "Leonardo will be with you in a moment. May I say, Mr. Adams, it is an honor to have you back with us."

Marc seemed embarrassed. His smile forced, he finally managed a "Thank you." The man bowed even lower this time and swept out the door. Heather watched with concealed amusement. She assumed the excess groveling was making Marc uncomfortable.

The two were alone in the room, the other two tables unoccupied. Heather leaned back in her chair and indulged in a favorite pastime of hers whenever she visited a new place, especially one loaded with antiques. She and her mother called it appraising. Her dad had another, harsher name for it, gawking, and he claimed nobody was more proficient at it than they were. She smiled, remembering his impatience with them, just as her eyes settled on still another chock-full china closet on the wall by the door with a claw-footed serving table right next to it. She would slip over and investigate those treasures more closely after they ordered, she decided. Everything was dark-stained oak, she noticed. The dining tables were sturdy, pedestal-type, and the chairs all high-backed with scroll-like designs worked into the richly grained wood. She ran a hand over the exposed surface of their table and could feel under her fingertips the subtle imperfections proper to a piece of furniture professing to be so old. *These are the genuine article,* she decided. *No modern antiques here.*

She looked across at Marc, ready to share her findings, only to find him staring into space, an odd look on his face. *Pensive* wasn't nearly strong enough to describe it, she decided. It was a thoughtful look, certainly, but there was a strained worry to go with it, a kind of pinched, pained expression, especially around the eyes. It bordered on panic. *I thought it was a little too quiet in here,* she thought. Aloud she asked, with a trace of concern in her voice, "Is something the matter?"

Her words brought him back, but he stared at her for just a split second as if he hadn't the slightest idea who she was. Then recognition returned, and his eyes reflected a kind of relief. The moment was downright chilling, as far as she was concerned. "I'm so sorry," he said. "I was a million miles away. Would you mind terribly if we went somewhere else?"

She tried unsuccessfully to keep the surprise out of her voice. "No, of course not. Whatever you want."

He knew he owed her some sort of explanation. "This place . . . it brings back some memories. We shouldn't have come here." He stood and came around the table to help her with her chair.

Suddenly Antonio's words echoed in her head—*I have your favorite table waiting*—and she understood. *This must have been* their *spot,* she thought. *But why would he take me here in the first place? He didn't know just how difficult it was going to be,* she decided as she preceded him back out the way they had come. *Shirley's right. This man is carrying a load of baggage.*

Antonio was at his post and turned in surprise as they came up behind him. "Mr. Adams, how may I help you?"

"Something's come up, Antonio," Marc said as he forced a bill into the man's hand. "I'm sorry; we have to go."

Antonio snapped his fingers at the coat-check girl, who hurried after their things. "Is something wrong, Mr. Adams? Leonardo was slow with the service, eh?"

"No, no, nothing like that," he assured the man. "We just remembered another engagement," he lied. "We'll be back another night."

Antonio's face brightened with a smile as he helped them with their coats. "Ah, very good. We will look forward to that. We have missed you at Antonio's, Mr. Adams." Suddenly he laid a hand on Marc's arm. "We were all so sorry for your loss. Yes, so sorry. But life must go on, eh? Yes, life must go on whether we like it or not. You have a good evening, my friend. And I hope we will see you soon."

"Thanks," Marc mumbled as the two stepped out into the cold, the snow falling faster now, the flakes smaller. "I'm sorry," he said as they neared the car. "I just couldn't handle that."

"It's all right," she said. She reached for his hand and took it in her own. "Let's walk. I love to walk in the snow." They set off then, with no destination in mind, walking toward the heart of the small town, leaving Antonio's behind. They walked for some minutes without a word, watching the snowflakes float by the streetlights as they passed.

"My wife and I used to go there all the time."

"I guessed as much."

"I haven't been back since it happened," he said. She could hear the crunch of their shoes in the snow before he added, "I haven't been much of anyplace since it happened. Just when I think I'm over it, something comes along to remind me, and I have to live through it all again. Like tonight." They walked some moments before he added, more to the falling flakes of snow all around them than to her, "Will it ever end?" Those words were filled with such pain that she felt the tears well in her eyes.

"I don't honestly know," she answered, and he looked at her quickly, realizing he'd actually spoken such an anguished thought. She knew enough about the grieving process to know that he had not allowed it to work within himself. He had pulled his whole world in on himself, keeping everything and everyone at bay with just one exception—his son. *If not for Jason, the man would have been lost altogether,* she decided. The boy had allowed him at least a foothold in the real world. *Why hasn't he talked this all out with someone?* she wondered. Aloud, she added, "But I *do* know you need to talk about it. It's not good to keep everything bottled up inside. Not good for you or for Jason."

They walked on. They were nearing the busy part of the town. Now they met shoppers in their bright ski clothes. "It's strange," he said finally. "People don't want to talk. I mean about things like death. I guess it makes them uncomfortable. We had lots of friends before, but they just kind of evaporated." They took a few steps in silence. "No, that's not true. I'm not really being fair. They came around at first. I guess you'd say they were very supportive, but they were good at changing the subject. The rule seemed to be not to mention Carole or little Karrie, like by mentioning their names I would suddenly remember the accident, when that's all I was thinking about anyway."

He said all this with no trace of bitterness in his voice. He was simply stating a fact. She knew only too well what he was talking about. She remembered a good friend in college whose fiancé drowned while kayaking only weeks before their wedding. Heather felt a pang of guilt when she remembered her awkwardness around this girl, her efforts to talk about everything under the sun except what her friend probably needed most to talk about. She glanced at Marc, wondering what his life was like before, what *he* was like. Jess had said he had been heavily involved in the community. What had happened to all that?

Almost as if he heard her silent questions, he went on. "I pulled back. I didn't go around with that crowd anymore. I felt like an extra wheel, and I could see in their eyes, or at least I thought I could, that they were uncomfortable with me around. So I became a bitter, cantankerous man." He emphasized the words, and at some sound of denial from her he added, "No, it's the truth. Ask anybody around town, and they'll tell you. Some of those old friends tried to get back inside. I can't deny that. But I locked them out and threw away the key. I've become an expert at keeping the whole world out," he said. He almost added, "until you came along," but the thought surprised him almost as much as he knew it would surprise her, and he smothered the words while they were still in his throat.

"What about Jason?"

"I can't imagine the way I've been existing has done him any good, but he's been my lifeline. I never would have made it if it hadn't been for him. I worry about him all the time, though. I'm afraid he's lost two years of his life because of me."

"I think you can stop worrying about him. Youngsters are pretty resilient. He knows how much you love him. There are a lot of them out there who never get that love. If you want my professional opinion, he seems to be a bright, well-adjusted little boy."

"Thanks to you. You should have seen him last year."

"He's just turned the corner. He'll be fine now," she assured him.

The two, hand in hand, had just trudged in the snow through the very heart of Keats, oblivious of everything going on around them. Marc stopped suddenly and turned to Heather. He was feeling much better now. "Do you realize we're about a mile from the car?"

"Uh-huh."

There was worry etched on his face. "Your knee. I forgot about your knee. You just got rid of your crutch, and we're tramping all over town."

She smiled. "It's feels fine. Really. The doctor said I was supposed to exercise it anyway."

"I know, but a mile in the snow?" He looked down at her feet. "And in shoes like that."

"What's wrong with my shoes?"

"Nothing, but they weren't made for mountain climbing."

She studied her feet. "You just might have a point."

"You must be freezing. And probably hungry too."

"If you want to know the truth, I'm starved." She grinned at him. "And I haven't felt my toes for the last half hour."

"Here I've been carrying on about myself a mile a minute. We need to get you warm." He looked around him to get his bearings. "Fazio's is only half a block up from the corner we just passed. They've got the best pizza in town. Does that sound okay?"

"That sounds wonderful."

* * *

Fazio's was busy and noisy, but they managed to find a high-backed booth in a corner. Heather had to admit the pizza was good, New York style, just the way she liked it. The two were outlandishly overdressed for the place, but no one seemed to notice, and Marc and Heather wouldn't have cared even if they had. If what Marc needed most was to talk, he got his therapy that night. He talked as he hadn't for years, and Heather was a perfect listener. They sat across from each other for what seemed like hours and left only when they finally caught a hint from the waitress that there were lots of people waiting at the door.

Afterward they made their way back to the car through three inches of snow, and it was still falling. Heather was thankful she hadn't opted for her really high heels, while admitting that her hiking boots would have been a better choice. Marc drove slowly back to her condo. He walked her to the door, and the pair stood on the steps, flakes of snow drifting around them. "I'm sorry about dinner."

"Don't be," Heather said. "The pizza was delicious."

"We'll try Antonio's another night, I promise. I know you'll like it."

"I liked the antiques. And Antonio was charming."

"Antonio must think I'm nuts."

"I thought you handled it very well."

"Thanks." He looked down at her with a touch of nervousness. "Thanks for listening." He bent and kissed her then, a light, gentle kiss that even for its abruptness still gave her a quick chill of excitement up her spine. "Good night. I hope you didn't ruin your shoes." He turned and walked quickly to his car, waiting until she had closed her door before driving off. He drove slowly home, wondering why he should be feeling so good after the way he had ruined their evening.

Heather stepped into the warmth of the living room, surprised to see Shirley working at the dining-room table. "What are you doing home?" she called as she pushed the door closed with her hip and struggled out of her coat. "What time is it, anyway?"

Shirley pushed her coloring project aside and stretched. She took a long swallow of Coke. "What happened? Did you lose track of time or did your watch stop?"

Heather slipped her shoes off at the door and padded to the table. She sat down across from Shirley. "You were right the first time. The night just flew by after a kind of shaky start."

"Well, don't keep me in suspense. Tell me all about it."

"You first. You're home awfully early, and what's this?" she asked pointing at the papers on the table. "You're working? And on a Friday night, no less?"

Shirley shook her head. "I know. It is kind of disgusting, isn't it? You must be having a bad influence on me." She sighed. "We did go out—for fast-food chicken, if you must know." A look of disgust accompanied her tone. "I swear Erik is like a man possessed when it's snowing. He wants to get up at dawn tomorrow to go skiing on fresh powder, so he went home early to see about having his skis waxed. Now, isn't that the most romantic thing you've ever heard? I like to ski, but don't you think that's carrying it just a little too far?"

"It's a guy thing," Heather said with a grin.

"Yeah, I suppose you're right." She stared off into space with a little pout on her lips. "Here I was choking down greasy chicken, and you were schmoozing with the jet-setters at Antonio's."

"Not quite."

"What? No big names there tonight?"

"I wasn't there long enough to find out." Shirley's face showed her surprise as she stared at Heather across the table. So Heather had to tell the whole story about leaving Antonio's early. Then she told about the long walk in the snow and the serious marathon conversation at Fazio's. Shirley was also a good listener. Her years as a first-grade teacher had trained her for that. Her dark blue eyes were always so expressive that she couldn't have hidden her emotions even if she wanted to. The two sat in silence for a moment when Heather had finished. "That's so sad," Shirley said finally. "I mean about leaving the restaurant and all. It must have been horrible for him. What did you say, anyway?"

"I didn't really say anything except that it was okay. What else *could* I say?"

"Yeah, you're right." She took another drink of Coke. "I told you it wasn't going to be all smooth sailing with him. But you got him talking. That's good. That's what he's needed for a long time.'' She raised her eyebrows in a questioning look. ''Doesn't he have any family to talk things out with? Mother and father? Brothers or sisters?''

Heather shook her head. ''No. He said he was an only child. His folks married late. I gather there was quite an age difference between his mother and father. His dad died when Marc was like four or five, I think he said, and then his mother died just six years ago of cancer.''

''That's rough. What about his late wife's folks? Any support there?''

''They live way back in Connecticut. They arranged for Jason to fly there this past summer and the one before for a week. Marc just about doesn't exist as far as they're concerned. He's invited them to visit, but they won't.''

''He is isolated, isn't he?''

''Yes, and I told you what he said about their friends. I know people don't mean to ignore you at times like that. They just don't know what to say. I've been there myself.''

''Me too, I hate to admit.''

''And I'm certain he hasn't made it any easier. He's not the kind of person who would go out looking for help, if you know what I mean. He would want to work it all out by himself. That's what he's been doing for the last two years, and look where it's gotten him.''

''That's the way most men are. I can see the same thing in Erik, that's for sure.'' Shirley leaned forward and rested her chin in her cupped hands in a reflective pose. ''You've got your work cut out for you, kid.'' She studied Heather for a moment. ''You really like him, don't you?''

''Yes, I do,'' Heather said simply. ''He's so gentle and sensitive once you get to know him. He sees things in such a different way. I guess that's the artist in him.'' Her voice filled with excitement as she went on. ''We found out tonight we think alike about so many things.''

''You did cover some ground, didn't you?''

Heather's smile faded. ''One huge problem, though.''

''Uh-oh, I knew it was too good to believe.''

Heather grinned. "He's a New York Yankees fan. I don't know if I can ever get used to that."

Shirley sat up straight and put her hands to her face in mock horror. "Oh, no, a Yankees fan. Whatever will you do?" She shook her head and took another sip of her Coke.

"Are there any more of those in the fridge?"

"I think so."

Heather went to the refrigerator and rummaged inside until she found what she was looking for. She sat down again and popped the tab. "I do have a problem, though. I mean a serious one this time."

Shirley had pulled her work toward her and was coloring again. "I'm almost afraid to ask, but what is it this time?"

"No, I'm serious. I don't know what to do about his wife. Carole was her name."

Shirley put her crayon down again. This was getting interesting. "What do you mean, what to do about her? There isn't much you *can* do about her, is there?"

"You know what I mean. If we got serious—and that's a very big if, mind you—how could I compete with someone he's still in love with?"

Shirley tapped her chin with a forefinger. "You've got to face facts. He's never going to forget his wife. She'll always be a part of their lives. She's Jason's mother, after all, and she always will be."

"Oh, I know all that. I wouldn't expect him to forget about her. How could I? But I don't like the idea that he's thinking of her all the time when I'm with him. Like he was doing tonight."

"He's not thinking of her all the time," Shirley said, but she wasn't positive she believed her own words when she said them. "You said yourself he's shut everyone else out for the past two years. He really stopped living when his wife and daughter died. Everything points to it—the personality change, the trouble with his painting, his social life. It's only natural he's obsessing over the past." She took a deep breath and thought for a moment, searching for the right words. "He got into a situation tonight that threw him back into the past."

"And tonight wasn't the first time, either."

"No, and it won't be the last. But look, if things work out, he'll begin thinking about you all the time. The two of you will have your own special places, special movies, special songs. Didn't you ever break up with someone and then just die when you heard your song on the radio?''

Heather nodded. ''I guess so.''

''Well, that's what he's doing. Only on a much bigger scale.''

''I suppose you're right.''

''Of course I'm right.''

Heather smiled. ''Time will tell. Hey, you know, you're good. Where'd you learn all that stuff?''

''Minor in psychology. I probably know just enough to be dangerous.''

''Well, what you say makes sense.''

''Now maybe we ought to start talking about my problems. Remember my so-called boyfriend would rather be back at the lodge having his skis waxed on Friday night than be with me.''

Heather laughed. ''Let's stick with my analysis tonight. We'll deal with you some other night when we have more time.''

''And just what is that supposed to mean?'' Shirley asked with an exaggerated glare. ''You think just because a thirty-year-old woman sits at home on a Friday night coloring a giant turkey that means there's something wrong with her?'' She twisted her face into a wild contortion and stared at Heather.

''No, I'd say you're about as sane as any first-grade teacher I've met.''

Shirley pulled the turkey toward her again and reached for a new color. ''And that isn't saying much, right?''

''You said it, I didn't,'' Heather added with a grin.

Shirley buried her head in her project. ''It'll all work out; don't worry.''

Heather stretched lazily and yawned. ''I suppose you're right. He's just a friend anyway.''

Shirley looked up from her coloring. ''Oh, sure,'' she said with a decided edge to her voice.

Chapter Eighteen

Marc stood at the living-room window, watching the snow-flakes swirl in front of him. He had just sent Becky Spooner off in her car after a strict warning to be extra careful. The roads were snowpacked and slippery. Becky was a good driver, he knew that, and she had four-wheel drive, which he made sure was engaged before she left, but he still worried. He no longer took cars for granted. Not since that day over two years ago. *What am I going to be like when Jason is old enough to drive?* he asked himself. He had checked in on him after Becky left. He was sleeping soundly, and Marc watched him for several minutes, comforted by the gentle rise and fall of the boy's chest and the peaceful look on his little face.

He stared into the blackness outside, his thoughts as varied as the white flakes that flashed by on the other side of the glass. *Why in heaven's name did I take her there, of all places? She was so understanding about that mess at Antonio's, but she probably thinks I'm some kind of head case.* He pictured her face, her dark eyes, the smile, always the smile. *That's what Jason noticed first,* he thought. "She smiles all the time, Dad," he had said after the first week of school. With an artist's memory for detail, Marc recalled what she was wearing tonight. *She was so dressed up,* he thought with another twinge of anger at himself. *I never even told her where we were going. So where do we end up? At a pizza place. And after walking miles in the snow.* He stared into the swirling snow without seeing it. *If I did portraits, I'd paint her in that dress, with that silver chain and those earrings. What were they?* He closed his eyes, trying to picture her again.

143

They were silver too. Now I remember. They were hoops, small ones.

He glanced at his watch. It was after eleven, but he wasn't in the least tired. A thought suddenly struck him. He walked quickly down the hall to the solarium and flicked on the lights. He headed straight for the easel waiting in the center of the room and gently removed the cloth covering the unfinished canvas. His paint box was on a shelf against the wall opposite the row of windows, and he dropped to one knee to retrieve it. His palette was on the top of the wooden box, and he frowned when he inspected it. It was covered with globs of dried paint from when he had last tried to work on this painting. He remembered he gave up that day in disgust. He snatched a plastic wastebasket from its place beside the computer desk, searched the paint box for his palette knife, and began scraping off the old paint. He looked down suddenly at his clothes and set the chore aside. He disappeared upstairs to his room to change into his favorite painting outfit—grungy sweatpants and sweatshirt. He checked on Jason again before returning to the studio to begin in earnest.

For the next several hours he lost himself in his work. His grandmother's apple orchard came to life again with each careful stroke of his brush. It had been a refuge, a place of love and security. He wanted it to be so much more than paint on a canvas. He had played among those trees, climbed those branches to reach the reddest fruit, built a fort just there where two trees twined together. He wanted her to see it. Wanted her to walk with him there as the nip in the air signaled the change of seasons.

A loud gust of wind rattled the wall of windows at his back, and Marc looked up suddenly from the canvas for maybe the first time in hours. He yawned and stretched, shaking his head, beginning to realize just how tired he had become. He glanced at his watch. Just after three. *No wonder I'm tired,* he thought. *It's a good tired, though. It feels so good to work like that again. To lose complete track of time. I haven't been able to do that in years.* He stood stiffly and stepped several paces away from the easel to get the full view of his canvas. He smiled. *Not bad. Not bad at all. It still needs some work, but I'd better not try to do it all in one night. I get sloppy if I get too tired.* He dug in his paint box until he found what he was looking for—a roll of plastic wrap. He tore off a generous piece and wrapped it carefully over the top of his palette to keep his mixed paints from drying out this time. He took another long look at the painting and nodded his satisfaction before turning off the lights and going up to bed.

Chapter Nineteen

The phone rang Saturday afternoon just as Shirley was going out the door in her bright yellow ski outfit. "I'll get it," she shouted. "It might be Erik. If he backs out of our ski date, I'm going to kill him." She picked up the receiver. "Hello. Yes, she's right here. Just a second." She held her hand over the receiver. "It's Marc. Or should I say Mr. Adams?"

Heather sprang off the couch as if her ski injury were no more than a distant memory. "Just never you mind." She snatched the phone. "Hello." Shirley backed toward the door, making kissing sounds on the back of her hand.

"Hi," he said, his voice deep and clear over the phone. "No aftereffects of our long walk in the snow?"

Heather laughed. "No, none at all, I'm happy to report."

"That's good. I was afraid your knee might be giving you trouble. We must have walked a good two miles."

"Nope, no problem," she said brightly. "I really think I'm going to be back skiing before you know it."

"Great." There was a long silence. "I was wondering, I mean if you're not doing anything, if you'd like to try it again next Friday. Not the skiing. I mean going out to eat. I guarantee it'll be a nice place this time. No pizza."

"The pizza was good. I'd been wanting to try Fazio's anyway. Sure, I'd love to go out Friday. What time?"

"How about seven? Will that work for you?"

"Sounds perfect."

"Okay, seven it is. See you then. 'Bye now."

"Bye-bye," she answered.

Heather hung up the phone and smiled. She could tell just how nervous he was, and she thought it was cute. She was relieved Shirley had left. All she needed was to have that bright yellow pixie dancing around the kitchen, making obnoxious faces at every word she said over the phone.

Marc placed the receiver in its cradle and dried the palm of his hand on his jeans. *That was short and sweet,* he thought to himself. *I think my telephone small-talk needs a little work.* He groaned aloud. *Is this going to get any easier?* he asked himself.

Friday's date was a regular topic of conversation for the two roommates during the week. Even Heather was calling it a date by now, in deference to Shirley's definition. "The first time out maybe, just maybe, I could stretch a point and say it was just a meeting of two friends," she said, "but I think even that sounds pretty lame. The second time out, that's a date, plain and simple. Even your mother would agree to that."

"Are you kidding? My mother would call it a date if a guy gave me a ride home from work. On the second date she's already checking when the church is available."

Shirley giggled. "She's the marrying kind, I gather?"

"Yes, she's impossible. She's seems to have a mortal fear of her daughter's being an old maid, as she calls it."

"I've got to meet this woman. She sounds like a kick."

"You'll get your chance. She and my dad will be pulling in here just when we least expect them. I'm surprised my dad has stayed away from the ski slopes this long, but he's been working really hard, according to what Mom says. I'm worried about him. I don't understand why he can't ease up a little. When I go home for Christmas, I'm going to talk some sense into the two of them. It's silly for me to be out here in the middle of the mountains and not have them visit."

"Amen," Shirley added. "We've got plenty of room here, and remember there's Erik and his free lift tickets," she said with a lilt to her voice. "Don't forget about that."

Friday night couldn't have been more perfect. Not only was Heather looking forward to her date with Marc, but it was the weekend before Thanksgiving and she was getting more than a little anxious for the short break from school the holiday would provide. She wouldn't be going back to St. Louis. The distance was simply too great for just four days. Shirley would be off to Denver to visit friends and had begged Heather to come along, but she declined. She knew Jess would call with an invitation for turkey dinner, probably at the last minute. She guessed that her cousin had forgotten to call, or maybe she thought an invitation was unnecessary, since Heather had spent the day with them the last several years while she was living in Denver. St. Louis was a long drive from Denver, and Heather always saved her flying money for Christmas. She never missed a chance to go home then. She checked her face in the mirror one last time. *Even if I'm here by myself,* she thought, *it won't be all bad. I can sleep late and just take it easy all day.* But deep down she had to admit that wasn't her ideal way of enjoying such a family holiday.

The sound of the doorbell broke through her thoughts. She answered the door wearing her trustworthy little black dress, good for all occasions. It was a trim, to-the-knee affair with a scoop neckline, and it never failed to make her feel chic. Tonight she had even opted for the exquisite antique diamond pendant given to her by her grandmother. It rested delicately at the hollow of her throat. And she wore the diamond earrings that came close to matching the necklace. She had found them at an antique-jewelry store in Denver. The diamonds were minuscule, but the earrings went so well with the pendant. The total effect, Heather knew, was a bit dressy for Keats, where, she was learning, casual always seemed to be in style, but tonight she just didn't care. She felt like dressing up, and when she watched Marc's eyes widen as she pulled open the door, she knew she'd made the right choice.

They tried a French restaurant called simply Le Bistro. Marc admitted he had never been there before, and considering what had happened the week before, Heather was relieved at that news. The food was delicious and the service elegant. Afterward they went to a trendy saloon just on the edge of town that featured live entertainment. The Glass Bottom Boats were in town and had been packing them in, from what Heather had read in the local newspaper. *Packing them in* was no exaggeration, she discovered. She and Marc were lucky to get in the door, and squeezed around a table only slightly larger than a medium-size pizza. Now Heather did feel overdressed, surrounded by a sea of jeans and leather and cowboy hats and bright ski clothes. She tried to tell that to Marc but discovered she had to shout to be heard over the din in the place, and the Boats weren't even on-stage yet.

He waved his hand in dismissal. "Don't worry about it. They'll think you're some movie star."

"Oh, right. Like that's going to happen."

He grinned across at her. "That's what I thought when you opened the door tonight. I was afraid I'd gotten the wrong address."

She eyed him and raised an eyebrow. "Uh-huh."

He pulled to a stop in front of her condo and turned off the engine. "So what did you think of the Boats?"

"They were great. How about you?"

"I liked them too." He tapped the side of his head with the palm of his hand in the manner of a diver clearing his ears of water. "But I've got the darnedest ringing in my head."

"Me too. You know we're going to have hearing loss by the time we're forty-five."

"What's that?" he asked with his hand cupped to his ear.

"Oh, you." She laughed.

He had turned slightly in his seat to face her, and he leaned his head against the cold glass of the side window. "Seriously, I just read an article about that in the paper. Maybe we ought to wear earplugs when we go to a live concert."

The thought struck her as funny, and she laughed with that little giggle that he was beginning to find so irresistible. "We'd look real cute, sitting there with our earplugs in."

He grinned sheepishly. "Well, it was just a thought." He tapped the steering wheel nervously with a forefinger. "I was wondering . . ." His voice trailed off.

Heather waited for him to finish. "Yes?" she asked finally.

"I was wondering what you were planning to do for Thanks-giving. I mean, are you going back to St. Louis or what?"

"No, I won't be going home till Christmas. It's just too far." She leaned back against the headrest. "Oh, I don't know. I guess I'll go to my cousin Jess's."

"Oh, I see."

Something in his tone made her add quickly, "But she hasn't really asked me yet, to tell you the truth. I think she just assumes I'll be there. Why do you ask?"

He raised his eyes hopefully. "We, I mean Jason and I, were just wondering if you'd like to have Thanksgiving dinner with us."

She turned her head toward him in surprise. She smiled, and her eyes suddenly flashed mischievously. "Hot dogs and baked beans?"

He laughed. "No, I'd be in charge of the cooking, if you wouldn't mind helping out a little. There's nothing to roasting the turkey, but I haven't got a clue about how to make gravy."

"Gravy is my specialty."

"Then you'll come?"

"Sure, why not? Jess won't miss me this one time. It sounds like fun."

"I warn you; we always watch football after dinner."

"Well, I would hope so. That's what the Pilgrims did, didn't they?"

Marc could barely hide his relief. "Great. Jason will be excited. We'll eat about one o'clock, if I can figure out what time to put the bird in so he'll be done by then. Why don't you come about eleven-thirty or so? That'll give you plenty of time to fix whatever we've done wrong."

Heather smiled. "Eleven-thirty it is. Now I think I'd better get in before my hands and feet freeze solid."

"I'm sorry. I should have left the car running. I wasn't thinking." He hopped out and hurried around to help her with her door.

The two walked to the front step, and she turned to him as she fumbled for her key. "I had a wonderful evening. Thanks so much."

He leaned down and kissed her hurriedly, nervously. "Good night. See you Thursday." He turned and walked quickly back to his car. Heather pushed open the door and stepped into the warmth of the apartment, a strange tangle of thoughts at work in her head. She *did* have a wonderful evening, she thought as she hung up her coat. Marc was fun to be with. They enjoyed many of the same things. He was smart and clever and funny. And she liked his serious side too. She was certain that he liked her, but still, there was the problem she'd discussed with Shirley. At times, the man just disappeared off into space somewhere. She didn't know if she could ever get past that barrier between them. Shirley's words came back in a flash: *It isn't going to be all smooth sailing,* she had said. Heather shook such thoughts from her head. She liked him a lot. She just knew he felt the same about her. *I've just got to give him time to come to grips with his past, that's all,* she decided.

Chapter Twenty

But giving Marc time to deal with his past would prove more difficult than Heather ever could have guessed. Not that she had much time to dwell on such somber thoughts for the moment. She was too busy trying to contain the excitement of twenty-six students for the holiday to finally come. Those three school days before Thanksgiving seemed like they would go on forever. And the bad part was that their anticipation was catching. She couldn't help but feel it herself. After all, it had been ages since the school year started, or at least it seemed that way to her.

Shirley was being a little too cute about the Thanksgiving dinner invitation. "Okay," she started off Monday on the way home from school, "I figured this all out during lunchroom duty. A regular invitation out to a restaurant is worth one point. An invitation to his home for dinner is worth five points." She glanced toward Heather to see how she was taking all this. "Now, I'm not counting the hot-dogs-and-beans deal because he didn't know anything about it. But a holiday invitation is a whole different ball game. I'm going to give it at least a ten." She slapped the steering wheel for emphasis.

Heather gave her a withering look. "So what's your point?"

"Oh, nothing really," Shirley said lightly. "Just making conversation."

Heather eyed her suspiciously. "Uh-huh."

Then there was trouble with Jess, as Heather knew there would be. She finally got around to calling with a Thanksgiving invitation, only to find out her favorite cousin had other plans. Heather knew Jess wasn't really upset, though she liked to pretend she was. When she found out where Heather was going, her voice got that ''knowing'' tone to it. *Honestly,* Heather thought, *she's as bad as Shirley.* Wednesday finally crawled to an end, and Heather sighed with relief as she watched her twenty-six nine-year-olds stream out the door ready to explode with their pent-up energy. They could be a joy at times, but this week didn't happen to be one of those times. She smiled to herself as she imagined the change in those smiling faces come Monday morning.

The two carpoolers hurried home right after school. Shirley was anxious to get on the road to Denver before it got too dark out, and Heather helped her pack the car. She watched as the car pulled out the drive onto the highway toward town. She hurried back inside, shivering against the cold. The condo was warm and cozy, and she dropped into a chair, happy with the thought that she had the entire evening to herself to do whatever she pleased. She stretched out on the couch, relishing the unaccustomed quiet, and allowed herself to think about the next day. She smiled when she imagined Marc bumbling his way around that big kitchen of his trying to get things ready for Thanksgiving dinner. *That's not fair,* she thought. *He might be the greatest cook in the world, for all I know.* Suddenly she laughed out loud. *But I seriously doubt it.* An idea struck her. *I bet he hasn't even thought about dessert. Why don't I whip up one of my fabulous pumpkin pies and surprise him?* She pulled herself up with renewed purpose and headed for the kitchen.

On Thanksgiving morning Heather slept late, lounged around in her robe, and watched the Macy's parade on television as she ate her breakfast. When she finally got around to checking the clock, she realized she would have to hurry to make the Adamses' home by eleven-thirty. After a quick shower, she tugged on a pair of jeans and pulled on a Keats Elementary sweatshirt, the one with the eagle mascot emblazoned on the front. She grabbed her coat and was halfway to the car before she remembered the pumpkin pie.

She pulled into the Adamses' driveway just a few minutes past eleven-thirty. Jason opened the door before the doorbell chime had faded away. He shouted excitedly when he saw the pie

Heather was carrying. "Dad, don't worry about dessert. Miss DeLaney brought pie."

Heather laughed and handed it to him. She slipped out of her coat. "I *thought* you two might have forgotten."

"We remembered about fifteen minutes ago," Marc shouted from the kitchen. He appeared at the kitchen door, and Heather had to clamp her hand over her mouth to hold back a squeal of laughter at the sight of him, a white apron cinched around his slim waist. "I saw that," he said with a grin. He looked down at the apron. "At least I can look the part." He inspected the golden brown pie as Jason carried it almost ceremoniously past him. "Put it on the counter there, buddy. Oh, that looks delicious, doesn't it? We were just about ready to check the fridge for Popsicles. We're not used to these big productions." He stepped toward her. "Here, let me hang up your coat."

She handed it over and took a long sniff of the air. "It smells like the turkey is about done."

Jason had rejoined them. His dark eyes were flashing with excitement. "The little red thing hasn't popped out of him yet."

Marc smiled. "It will, son. Just give it time." He turned to Heather. "Can I get you a glass of wine, a soft drink? Or I have hot apple cider."

"Oh, that sounds good. Some cider, please."

"One hot apple cider, coming right up."

"Miss DeLaney, will you play a game of Death Rockets with me?" Jason pleaded.

Marc wrapped his arms playfully around the boy. "Jason, she just got here. Let's save that for after dinner."

"Okay, but I've been practicing."

"Hey, that's not fair," Heather said with a grin. "You beat me bad enough last time, and now you've been practicing."

Jason's smile was positively impish. "I'll go easy on you. I promise."

"Okay, you'd better." She turned to take a look out of one of the tall windows by the fireplace. The day was crisp, the sky a deep blue. She could see the snowcapped mountains clearly in the distance. "What a fantastic view," she murmured aloud, but to herself. Marc and Jason had gone back to the kitchen. She followed to see if there was anything she could do and caught a peek of the turkey as Marc checked the timer.

"Still hasn't popped," Jason announced.

Marc slid the roaster back into the oven. "Remember, a watched timer never pops," he said with a grin.

"Oh." Heather groaned. "That was so bad." She checked her watch and announced in a solemn voice, "Okay, based on my years of successful turkey roasting, I'm making a prediction." She pointed at the oven. "The timer on this bird will pop in exactly thirty minutes. Synchronize your watches."

Jason could hardly contain his excitement. "I bet it won't. If you're wrong, you have to play me two games of Death Rockets. No, three games."

"It's a deal," she said, "on one condition. You can't be looking every three minutes."

"Not even in the window?" he protested.

She folded her arms. "No. Remember what your dad said. A watched timer never pops."

"Oh, that's not true."

Heather winked at Marc. "Do we have a bet or not?"

"Okay," Jason said, "but I get to say when the time is up."

"Agreed." The two shook hands.

They continued with the rest of the meal preparations, but Jason was no help at all. He was too busy watching the clock. "Time," he shouted finally as the red second hand touched the twelve on the clock over the sink.

They gathered around the stove as Marc slowly opened the oven door and slid out the rack supporting the roaster. The red plastic timer was clearly visible. "Yes!" Heather shouted, clinching her fist in front of her for all the world like Tiger Woods sinking a long putt.

"Aw," Jason moaned. He crumpled to the tile floor near the refrigerator. "How did you know that dumb timer would pop out in thirty minutes?" Suddenly his eyes brightened and he jumped to his feet. "Hey, no fair. How do you know it didn't pop a long time ago after Dad put the turkey back?" The full realization that he'd been had swept over his face. "That's why you wouldn't let me check in between, bet."

Marc chuckled at the two as he hoisted the turkey out of the roaster and onto a cutting board. Heather put her arm around the boy's shoulder and playfully tousled the shock of red hair. "Right. Now because you figured it out so fast, I'll still play you a game of Death Rockets."

He looked up at her, his eyes pleading. "Two? Please?"

"No, just one . . . unless I beat you. Then I'll play you again to give you a second chance."

He pirouetted away, giggling at the thought. "You, beat me? That's a good one, Miss DeLaney. I bet I could win with my eyes shut."

Heather was adding flour to the roaster to start her gravy. "We'll see," she said, knowing he was probably right.

The dinner was delicious. The turkey was done to perfection. Heather's gravy was smooth and rich. Marc's mashed potatoes were a little thin—he had added just a touch too much milk. But he redeemed himself with his scalloped corn. It was done just right, with a light crust around the dish so you could get some of the delicious brownness with each spoonful. Heather was amazed that he would even tackle something so difficult, let alone succeed with it. Even the jellied cranberry sauce that had been Jason's responsibility was sliced into perfect circles—*wheels*, he called them. They talked easily between forkfuls of the feast about the upcoming football game; skiing; playing Monopoly; hikes they had done; school, of course. Jason gave an update on his Death Rockets scores. He was obsessed with the game, and Heather knew she wouldn't get away with just one round.

After the plates were cleared, Marc served generous portions of Heather's pumpkin pie. Jason smacked his lips and smiled after the first bite. "Um, good," he managed with his mouth full. He devoured his slice as if he hadn't already eaten two helpings of everything else on the table. Heather smiled as she watched him. She knew her mother would approve. She liked nothing better than seeing someone relish one of her home-cooked meals. Heather finished her own pie and pushed the plate aside. She leaned back in her chair and took a sip from her second cup of coffee, a feeling of warmth and comfort filling her.

She looked across the table at Marc and their eyes met. She would remember this moment later as the instant when she thought all was right with her world. But the moment lasted just that—a moment. Jason was collecting bits of pie crust from his plate with the tip of his forefinger and transferring them to his tongue, a sure sign that a nine-year-old was thinking deep thoughts. Suddenly he turned his dark eyes on his father. "Dad?" Something in the tone of his questioning voice made them both look at him. "Is this what Thanksgiving used to be like before Mom died? I try to remember, but I can't. Even when I close my eyes and think as hard as I can."

Marc stared at the boy, a look of surprise replacing the relaxed expression of just a moment ago. "I-I guess so," he mumbled after what seemed an eternity. He opened his mouth as if to say more, but no sound came out. Instead he stared out the window into the foothills behind the house.

"Did Mom fix turkey and punkin pie and stuff too?" the boy persisted.

Thinking back, as she drove home that afternoon, about the abrupt ending to such a promising day, Heather suddenly saw how unavoidable it actually had been. On a day set aside specifically for family, they had avoided even the slightest reference to anything *about* family. Surely that was no accident, she decided. She had to admit that she hadn't even mentioned past holidays at home lest they should remind Marc of his horrible loss. And this coming from the person who had actually convinced herself that she was good for the man, when she was the biggest enabler of all. She gritted her teeth in anger at herself. But if there was some kind of implied agreement not to bring up anything about past holidays, with all their warmth and love and family, then clearly Jason hadn't been in on it.

What had happened after dinner was downright bizarre. The three worked together to clear the table and load the dishwasher, but it was plainly obvious Marc was somewhere else again. If spoken to, he answered in monosyllables. His tone couldn't be interpreted as sullen or angry, just preoccupied and almost robot-like. Heather tried her best to turn his mind to the present, but to no avail. And Jason? He jabbered on nonstop through the scraping and clattering of dishes, oblivious of how his earlier questions had dampened the moment.

After the work was done, Heather excused herself with a little half-truth. She was expecting a call from her family. They always talked by phone on a holiday when they were apart, she said. The truth was that she would make the call herself, and not until evening, when the St. Louis crowd was recovering from their traditional late-afternoon dinner. The look of disappointment on Jason's face almost brought tears to her eyes. He had been counting on more rounds of Death Rockets and then the football game. As a matter of fact, so was she—even the Death Rockets. But Marc went to retrieve her coat from the closet without one word of protest. He forced a smile and thanked her for coming, but his heart wasn't in it.

As she pulled off Highway 17 onto Rayburn Road, Heather's anger suddenly fixed on a target other than herself. *What is wrong with that man?* she thought, even though she knew full well the answer. *Didn't he invite me? And then to be treated like I practically wasn't even there. It's about time he starts looking at the future instead of the past before he ruins that little boy. I was practically kicked out the door.* Her anger faded when she remembered that her quick exit was really her own doing. *Well, what was I supposed to do?* she reflected. *Stay around and be ignored?*

She drove on, unaware that a front of dark clouds was just starting to push over the mountains. The clouds hadn't yet reached the sun. She smiled in spite of herself at the thought of her timer trick on Jason. Then she remembered Marc's eyes across the table—such dark, gentle eyes. Had she seen more in that look than he intended? She didn't think so. But when she remembered the change in those eyes at the innocent questions of the boy, she felt the tears well in her own eyes. She knew she would do anything to ease the pain he was feeling at that moment. She vowed then and there to talk with him. He needed to learn to put the past gently to rest if there was hope for a future.

Chapter Twenty-one

It was the day after Thanksgiving, and Marc was trying to work at his downtown gallery. He was alone. Jason had left early to go ice-skating with a friend, and Doris and Becky had the day off. The gallery, technically speaking, would be open today, but Marc wasn't expecting much business. He knew he could handle any visitors from his loft perch. He had been staring at the canvas in front of him for the past half hour without making a single brushstroke.

He couldn't stop thinking about yesterday and how he, all by himself, had turned such a promising day for all three of them into a total disaster. When he finally came to his senses after Heather left, he discovered just how disappointed Jason was. The boy sulked around the house for the rest of the day. He didn't even have much appetite for turkey sandwiches, always a favorite, and he hardly looked at the big game on television. Marc had been so busy feeling sorry for the boy that it didn't dawn on him until late last night, when the little guy had gone off to bed, just how much he really missed her himself.

Yes, he'd done a lot of thinking last night. He'd been a fool. Yesterday, yes, but not just yesterday. There were other times too, when he ruined the moment thinking about the past. *Maybe it's a good thing yesterday happened,* he decided. It made him realize what he could lose. Because the truth was that he hadn't been able to get Heather out of his mind for two minutes at a stretch since yesterday. *Since yesterday?* he thought with a grimace. *More like since I first saw her that day at school.* He rolled his eyes when he remembered that day. *I was in rare form, wasn't I?* He shook his head in disbelief. *How long ago was that? It*

159

doesn't seem possible that it's been only three months. So much has happened. So much.

He knew it was finally time to climb out of the pit of depression he'd been wallowing in for the past two years. That point had finally sunk into his head late last night as he listened to the November wind howl through the pines around the house. *Life will never be the way it was,* he thought. *But then it never is. Things change. Not always as horribly as they did for us two years ago, but they still change. Now, what to do?* He leaned forward and slapped the paintbrush on the lip of the easel in a gesture that showed a sudden resolve. He had really made up his mind last night, but it had taken until now to put those thoughts into a plan of action. *I'll never forget Carole and the baby,* he thought. *But nobody said I have to. Jason needs to remember them too. I've got to stop shutting him out like I did yesterday.* The next words he spoke aloud, and the sound of his own voice echoing through the high-ceilinged gallery surprised even him. "I've been shutting out Heather too, and it's going to stop, starting this minute."

He smiled as he stood and stepped to the telephone. A weight had been lifted. He knew it was over for good—those long days and nights of mourning. It was about time he stopped punishing those around him, even those he loved. He was alive. More alive than he had been for so long. He hadn't died in that crash two years ago, even though there had been times when he wished he had. No more. Finally he was seeing things clearly. He wasn't positive how Heather felt about him. He thought he knew. He hoped he knew, but whatever, he was about to find out—to find out if there really was a chance for them. He picked up the phone and dialed her number.

Heather spent a restless night. She watched each hour come and go in glowing red on her bedside clock radio as she tossed and turned. Her sleep was fitful, and her dreams endless and muddled. With a groan of resignation, she threw the covers off and crawled out of bed just a few minutes after six. She sat on the edge of the bed, bleary-eyed. She never got up at such an hour if she didn't have to. She dragged herself across the room and into the bathroom, and stared at herself in the big mirror over the sink. She wasn't happy with what she saw—hair sticking out in all directions and eyes bloodshot and puffy.

She dressed quickly, pulling on her dark blue sweats, including the zip-up top with a hood. She had decided to go for a long hike after breakfast, and it took no more than a glance out her bedroom window to tell her the day was overcast and gloomy. *It figures,* she thought. She was certain a good hike would help sort things out. A marathon of mind-numbing television at home yesterday after her hurried exit from Marc's certainly hadn't helped. Not that she thought it would. After all, that was the idea—put her anger and frustration and worry as far away as possible. But not today. Today was a new day, and the one thing her night of tossing and turning had helped her decide was that it was about time to face reality, and what better way to do that than on a good walk? It had always worked before, and it would work today.

She picked at a breakfast of cold cereal, juice, and toast, then pulled on her heavy coat, tied the hood securely under her chin, yanked on her mittens, and headed out the door. She took the well-worn trail just behind the last condo in their development. It cut through a forest of spruce and lodgepole pine and meandered along a stream that had been a rushing torrent with melting snow from the high country when Heather first moved in, but today was little more than a trickle with ice and snow crusting its banks. She had hiked here a number of times on weekends and had even explored some of the higher climbs with trails branching from the main one, but not today. Today she would keep to level ground, coming out near the road by the front entrance, a distance of not much more than two miles.

It was cold. She exhaled little clouds as she walked, and she was grateful for the furry mittens that helped keep the chill at bay. She was also grateful that no one else was using the trail. She wanted to be alone. She needed to think. She allowed her mind to replay the events of Thanksgiving Day. A nagging thought had been gnawing at her ever since her quick departure yesterday. Had she overreacted? She knew she had probably ruined the day for Jason. She had promised to spend the afternoon, and it was obvious he had been looking forward to her being there. He needed family things, and maybe that was what she had provided. Hadn't his questions at dinner suggested as much?

No, she decided. *I did the right thing. What else could I do? The man practically ignored me. I've had it.* A wave of anger churned her insides. She had been trying too hard to bottle up that anger since yesterday, and now it spilled out. *A person ought to be able to at least mention his wife's name without bringing on some kind of trauma.* She tried to ignore a feeling that swept through her then, a feeling she had first recognized on the way home yesterday. *I'm jealous of her. I'm actually jealous of a woman who's been dead for two years. How in the world could that be? That is the most horrible thing I've ever heard of.*

She walked on as her thoughts disintegrated into a jumble of shame and guilt. How long she had been on the trail she wasn't certain. She continued, almost mechanically, on the worn path that stretched before her. Her footfalls suddenly sounded hollow on a portion of the trail that cut close to the stream, and the odd sound brought her back to the present. She glanced about at a small grove of aspen nestled among the pines and saw, without really seeing, fresh elk damage where the long-legged, shaggy animals had stretched their heads high along the slender trunks to gnaw at the tender bark.

She forced herself to think things through. *It's just not going to work, that's all there is to it. He's not going to be able to forget her. I have no right to expect that he should. Maybe there's something wrong with me, but I just can't deal with this whole thing. It's like I'm competing with someone who isn't there, someone who probably will always be perfect in his mind. That's a no-win situation if I ever heard of one.* She let out a deep sigh, and all her anger left her.

Tears stung her eyes, but she smiled as she thought of him. She remembered the touch of his hand holding hers as they waited in the cold snow of the ski slope for help. His voice, warm and comforting. The frightened look in his eyes as he watched her. She had always dreamed of such a man, caring and protective yet strong and sure, to share her future. She shook her head from side to side as if to sweep those thoughts away. *This is stupid. We've known each other all of three months. What makes me think I could ever take his wife's place? I was wrong to think I ever could. He must have loved her very much.* When she realized what she had to do, the tears began in earnest.

At that moment she broke out of the trees by the road, surprised to see she had made the full circuit of the trail, but if she needed any convincing she had walked over two miles, the cold creeping into her boots and the tingling of her nose and tear-stained cheeks did that convincing. She hurried forward to the warmth of the condo. Once inside, she peeled off her mittens and coat, undid her hood, and went to the kitchen to go through the motions of brewing a fresh pot of coffee. She carried the steaming cup to her favorite chair and tried to lose herself in a book, but she kept reading the same page over and over. She had decided what she would do. Usually that made her feel better, but not today. The book slipped out of her hands as tears again blurred her vision. The phone rang.

She snatched a tissue from a box on the counter on her way to the phone and dabbed at her eyes. ''Hello.''

''Good morning,'' he said.

She felt a return of her anger at the matter-of-fact tone in his voice, as if nothing out of the ordinary had happened on Thanksgiving Day. ''Oh, it's you.''

''That's quite a greeting.'' He tried to make the words sound light, but they didn't come out that way.

''I just meant I wasn't expecting you to call.''

There was an awkward silence. ''I . . .'' He stammered getting his words out. ''I want to apologize for yesterday.''

''Oh, that's okay,'' she said. *Why am I letting him off the hook?* she asked herself, and then answered her own question with her next thought. *I can't tell him how I really feel over the phone.*

''No, it isn't okay. I always seem to be doing or saying something I need to apologize for.''

''You shouldn't be so hard on yourself,'' she said lamely.

There was another long pause. ''We need to talk.''

''I agree.''

Something inside him gave a little flip at the way she said those two simple words. It was almost the beginning of a new feeling of loss. ''Could I come over? I'm downtown. I can be there in ten minutes.''

Heather looked about her. *I don't want him to come here.* She didn't know why, but she thought it would be harder. "How about I come down there? I have a few errands to run," she lied. "I'll meet you at Brewer's Coffee House in, oh, say twenty minutes. Is that okay?"

"Fine. See you then." He hung up and stared over the railing of the loft at nothing in particular.

Heather parked her car downtown and hopped out. She had changed into jeans and a turtleneck sweater, and she had taken a few moments to try to do something with her face. The effect wasn't perfect, but she looked better. At least the puffiness around her eyes wasn't quite so prominent. She checked her watch. Late. She hadn't wanted to keep him waiting. As she rounded the corner just a half block from the Brewer's, she caught sight of him cutting across the street. He spotted her at nearly the same time.

"I was afraid you might not wait," he said in lieu of greeting. "Some folks came in just after I talked to you, and I didn't think they'd ever leave."

"You didn't have to worry. It takes me longer to drive down here than I thought." The two walked the half block side by side in silence.

Janis Nordway slipped behind the wheel of her car which was parked in a tow-away zone just outside Brewer's Coffee House. She had taken a chance on the parking, but she knew she would only be a minute. Just long enough to buy a bag of her favorite fresh-ground. She hurried just in case the local parking monitor was on the prowl. She clicked her seat belt and fumbled trying to fit the key in the ignition. Suddenly she froze with her hand on the key and stared through the front window. *Isn't that Miss DeLaney?* She was watching a couple walking together toward her. In an effort to avoid being seen, she tried to tuck her head into the collar of her heavy coat, for all the world like a turtle retreating to its shell, all the time keeping her eyes on the pair. Her lips tightened into a pucker. *And Marc Adams.* She clicked her tongue. *I thought there was something going on there.* Marc held the door for Heather and then followed her into the tiny coffee shop. Miss Nordway took a deep breath and straightened in the seat to her full height, a look of indignation on her face. She started her car and pulled away from the curb.

"Is a latte all right?" Marc asked.

Heather nodded and automatically headed for the table they had sat at before, the one near the front window. He went to the counter and placed their order, paid for their coffee, and brought the steaming cups to the table.

"This should hit the spot on a day like this," he said as he slipped into the chair across from her.

She took a sip. "This is what I needed after I came back from my hike this morning."

"You've been out already? You must be serious."

She smiled. Their eyes met for an instant and she looked quickly away. He felt his sinking feeling return and wondered why he had pushed for this meeting, forgetting for the moment what he had hoped to tell her. *It's probably too late anyway,* he thought when he remembered what he was there for. "Like I said on the phone," he began, "I'm sorry about yesterday. I don't know what came over me. I get into those moods sometimes, and nothing can drag me out. I know Jason was disappointed that you left. Not that I blame you, of course," he added quickly. "I know I wasn't fit company." *Go ahead,* he told himself, *tell her that things have changed. Tell her you can't stop thinking about her. Tell her that you think you love her. Tell her. Tell her!* he shouted at himself. But the thought of the stupid way he had acted yesterday kept those words stuck in his throat. He saw himself as she probably was seeing him just now, and the picture wasn't pretty. He took a drink of his latte. "You said we should talk."

"I didn't say it. You did. I only agreed."

"I guess I did. But you go first."

There was a long silence as they both studied the table. "Well," she began. She wasn't sure she could trust her voice. "I don't think we should see each other anymore." She hurriedly tried to wipe fresh tears from her cheeks with her fingertips, as if her action wouldn't be noticed.

He braved a quick glance at her and the sight of her red eyes and wet cheeks made his insides do a full flip. It was what he was afraid of from the tone of her voice on the phone. Could he have stopped those words if he had said what he wanted to? *Probably not,* he decided. He didn't know why he should be surprised. But when he heard the words he still was. "Why?" he asked, though when he said it, he wondered at his own stupidity for having asked such a question.

"Why?" she repeated, her voice rising to such a pitch that she glanced quickly at the back counter to see if they were attracting attention. Luckily there were no other customers in the shop. She lowered her voice, but the intensity was still there. "You ignore me like I'm not there, and you ask why?" She had managed to pull a tissue from her purse, and now she dabbed at her eyes.

He raised his head and saw her eyes again. He would rather face a ten-foot mountain lion than a woman's tears. "I said I was sorry," he mumbled.

"It's not enough just to keep saying you're sorry. Every time your wife's name is even mentioned, you fall into this, this . . . depression. The ski lodge, Antonio's, your house, everywhere—it's always the same. Don't you ever talk to Jason about his mother? He needs that, you know. And so do you. It would help you move on to the future instead of always thinking about the past." She sighed and shook her head. "I'm sounding like a schoolteacher."

"No, please go on."

"You won't want to hear the rest." She slid the nearly full coffee cup toward the center of the little table. "I feel like I'm being measured against your wife all the time. I know you don't mean to do it, but that's how it seems. Maybe if you talked about her more, I wouldn't feel so much that way. When you start your silent treatment, it's like there's a part of your life that you'll never let anyone know a thing about—even your son." The tears were starting again and she fumbled for her tissue. "Do you know you never really kiss me? Not like you mean it, anyway. Are you thinking of her then too? I can't be her. Don't you see that? I'm sorry, but I can't. I won't." She pushed away from the table, grabbed her purse, and bolted for the door. Marc made no attempt to stop her. He sat staring at the table. Out of the corner of his eye, he caught a glimpse of her as she hurried by the window.

Chapter Twenty-two

Shirley got back late Sunday afternoon. Heather had started a pot of fresh vegetable soup earlier in the afternoon, and it was simmering on the stove. Shirley dragged her suitcase through the door and sniffed the air. "Is that vegetable soup I smell?"

Heather smiled. "You have an uncanny nose for identifying cooking smells."

Shirley was hanging her coat. "I'm not brain-dead. Anyone can tell vegetable soup." She dragged her suitcase toward the hall. "I'm starved. All I had for lunch was a turkey sandwich, and I'm sick of turkey. Do you hear me? Sick! Sick! Sick!" She rolled her eyes.

Heather laughed as she stirred the thick soup before she started ladling it into bowls. "Well, sit down. I made a loaf of wheat bread too."

Shirley folded her hands prayerlike and looked toward the ceiling. "I've died and gone to heaven."

The two sat at their meal, and Shirley began, between spoonfuls of soup, a play-by-play description of her weekend that ran nearly nonstop for fifteen minutes. She explained in detail two new card games she'd learned, told about three exciting restaurants she'd tried, and narrated several stories involving her Denver friends. She finally slowed down and concentrated on her soup before it got cold. Suddenly her head came up. "Here I go, as usual, rambling on, and I haven't heard a thing about your Thanksgiving Day. So how was it? Tell me."

"To be honest, there isn't much to tell."

"I find that hard to believe."

"Well, I'm sorry, but it's the truth." So Heather told her story, but with none of the relish Shirley had displayed in telling hers.

"So you just ended it all?" Shirley asked in astonishment as Heather finished with the meeting at the coffee shop.

"Well, sort of."

"What do you mean, 'sort of'?"

"Well, I ran out in tears before I gave him a chance to say much of anything."

Shirley nodded. "Uh-huh. So this so-called breakup is pretty much one-sided as of right now?"

"I guess you could say that."

"And are you ever going to let him have his say?"

Heather pursed her lips. "I don't know."

"Well, I think you should. You're making a big mistake if you walk away. You two are perfect for each other."

"How can you tell that? We've only known each other for three months."

"I don't care if you've only known each other for three hours; I can tell. The way you two look at each other. Like that day when you had your skiing accident. If I didn't see two people in love that day, then I'll voluntarily turn in my license to meddle."

Heather smiled. "You're something else."

"I'm not kidding about this. Can you sit there and look me straight in the eye and tell me you don't feel something pretty special for Marc Adams?"

Heather hesitated. "No, I can't," she said quietly.

"Just as I thought."

"But there's still the problem with his late wife."

"We've been down this road before. I tell you, it's going to take time. He's been repressing for two years."

"Well, the ball's in his court. If he really cares about me, he'll do something."

" 'The ball's in his court,' " Shirley mimicked. "If you let him slip away, you're going to regret it." She saw the set of Heather's jaw just then and knew the subject was closed. At least for now.

Heather managed a smile at the somber faces before her Monday morning as she waited for the final tardy bell to ring. The scene was a far cry from the previous Wednesday, when it took all her skill to keep a lid on the place. Twenty-six kids were as low as the well-worn carpet on the classroom floor, and their teacher wasn't much better. Heather was in a foul mood all day. When she snapped at Leon Glenwood for tapping his fingers on his desktop, keeping time with some tune in his head, she saw eyes turn toward her in surprise. She had violated one of her own basic rules: reserve anger for those few times when it is absolutely necessary.

Heather and Shirley went home soon after the dismissal bell. Shirley promised her famous Moroccan dinner to lift their lagging spirits. Heather changed into jeans and a bulky sweater and announced she was going downtown to do some Christmas shopping. Shirley eyed her from her place on the sofa but said nothing.

Heather parked on a quiet side street and began to wander from shop to shop. The town was aglow with tinsel and lights and greenery, and every store had its own version of Christmas music. She bought a few things for those back home, but she had to admit her heart just wasn't in it. She pretended to drift aimlessly from window display to window display, but she knew deep down there was a purpose to her wandering. She turned the corner by Brewer's Coffee House, and she felt her heart beat faster. She strolled by as nonchalantly as she could manage and peered in the window at the table near the front, but no one was there. Then she crossed the street and continued up a block until she came to the boardwalk. She walked slowly past the co-op and then the gallery. Out of the corner of her eye, she saw Becky at her post, paperback in hand, while a handful of browsers moved from painting to painting in the back of the gallery.

She turned at the next corner and headed for her car, upset with herself. *What was I expecting?* she thought. *That I was just going to accidentally bump into him, and he would spout all those words of love Shirley was talking about? Yeah, something like that,* she thought as just the hint of a smile crossed her face. She hurried home, where Shirley's Moroccan dinner was well under way. But as delicious as it was, it made no headway at cheering Heather up, and the rest of the week continued as it had begun, with a certain fourth-grade teacher becoming increasingly impatient with a class unaccustomed to such treatment from their teacher.

Jason went from a teacher frayed at the edges, to a father grown suddenly glum. Gone this week was the usual joking between father and son at the gallery and around the dinner table. Jason put up with the silent treatment for three days. He didn't think his dad was mad at him. He wasn't snappish like Miss DeLaney at school, anyway. But still, the boy knew something wasn't right. He waited till Wednesday to say something. He had just finished his spaghetti, and he pushed the plate away. "Dad, are you mad or somethin'?"

Marc looked up. "No, why would you think that, buddy?"

"Cause you've been real quiet and stuff."

"I don't think I've been all that quiet."

"Uh-huh. You don't joke around like you used to." He stole a quick look at his dad. "Least you're not all grumpy, like Miss DeLaney."

Marc was suddenly interested. "You never said anything like that about Miss DeLaney before."

"That's 'cause it just happened this week. She even made us all stay in our room during gym 'cause the girls were talkin' during quiet time."

"Well, I'm sure she must have good reasons when she does those things."

"Uh-uh. She's just been real mean."

Marc twirled his last forkful of spaghetti with the help of his dinner roll and studied Jason's face as he mulled over this latest information. What his son said next took him by surprise. "Dad?"

"Yes?"

"I think Miss DeLaney would be a nice mom." Marc nearly choked on the last of his roll, which he had popped in his mouth. "Except I wouldn't like it if she got grumpy all the time." He thought for a second. "I don't think she'd be grumpy, though."

"Why not?"

" 'Cause she'd be my mom and she'd be married to you. I know she'd be real happy then."

"How do you know that?"

The boy smiled. "Oh, I just do." With that he slipped out of his chair and raced for the family room. "Dad, I'll pick up as soon as 'Kids from Outer Space' is over. Okay?"

Later that night after Jason was in bed, Marc had the peace and quiet to digest what he had heard at dinner. *So she's not having a good week. I know the feeling. It isn't over till it's over,* he thought. *I still might get her to listen to what I should have said the other day.* He checked the clock. *Too late to call tonight. I'll try her tomorrow, earlier.* He stretched back in his chair, feeling better than he had for days.

Chapter Twenty-three

Miss Janis Nordway arrived at her office even earlier than usual Thursday morning. She hadn't slept well. In fact, she hadn't slept well all week. She had been wrestling with a decision, and now she had finally made her mind up. She pulled the necessary transfer forms from her top desk drawer. *I could wait to make the change at the end of the semester,* she thought, *but no, I think it's better to take care of it now. It's an awkward situation. Miss DeLaney will be offended. And that Adams fellow. Have we ever done anything to suit him? Better this than have the whole town talking about preferential treatment.* She took a deep breath and began writing.

The bell sounded, and Heather stood to begin the day. She had vowed to keep her emotions on an even keel today. She had even switched to decaffeinated coffee last night and again this morning for breakfast. Maybe that would help. Last night she had made plans for a hands-on science experiment to study snow crystals under a microscope. She even came extra early to set up the equipment. Before she had a chance to begin, though, she noticed Miss Nordway standing in the doorway. Heather went toward her, a questioning look on her face.

"I need to see Jason Adams," she whispered.

Heather turned and motioned to him. "Jason."

He hopped out of his seat and joined them at the door, his eyes betraying just a trace of worry. No student at Keats Elementary welcomed a summons from the principal. It was definitely not a good way to start the day. Miss Nordway whispered in his ear, and he followed her out the door. Heather waited a moment before continuing with her lesson plans. She didn't want to go ahead without him, but he didn't return. She had no chance to check on him until the art teacher arrived at nine-thirty to take over. She helped her pass out supplies and then sneaked out and hurried to the office. Miss Nordway was at a meeting. Next she stopped at the staff lounge for a quick cup of coffee, decaffeinated again. Her hall neighbor, Jonas Slama, was just leaving.

"Who's got your class?" she asked.

"Student teacher," he answered. "She's flying alone in there for the first time, and I think I'd better get back." He started down the hall but stopped and turned before she had gone back into the lounge. "Say, what's the deal with the Adams boy?"

She froze with the door half open. "What do you mean?"

"Nordway just dropped him on me this morning. Said it was a special transfer, and I had the smallest class size. Has he been giving you trouble?"

A chill was making its way slowly up Heather's spine. "No, not at all. As a matter of fact, he's one of my best students."

Mr. Slama shrugged and adjusted his wire-rimmed glasses on his nose, a habit she'd seen students imitate. "Well, what do *we* know? We just work here. Right? I'll need to check with you about where he is in everything."

Heather let the door slam and took a few steps toward the other teacher. "Jonas, he's been through a lot. His mother and sister were killed in a car accident a couple of years ago."

"Oh, yeah, yeah, that's right," he said, nodding. "Now I remember. His dad gave Nordway fits the last couple of years. No trouble from the home front this year?"

"Not till now," Heather said.

"Well, don't worry," he assured her with a warm smile. "I won't undo any of your success." He gave a thumbs-up, spun around, and continued down the hall.

She let out a deep sigh. *So, Mr. Marc Adams is up to his old tricks.*

Heather had just returned to her desk after watching her class leave for the day. She had hoped to catch Jason in the hall to offer whatever consoling words she could, but he was nowhere to be found. Suddenly, just as she sat down, he slouched into the room, his heavy coat half on and half off. "Miss DeLaney, how come I got moved? Did I do somethin' wrong?"

"No, not at all," she assured him. "I don't know why you were changed. Maybe you should talk to your dad."

"Will you talk to him?"

"Well, I don't know if I can do that."

"Why not?"

"Your dad and I think it's better if we don't see each other for a while."

He stared at her with his big brown eyes. "Don't you like him anymore?"

"I didn't say that. It's just that, well . . . maybe you'd better talk to your dad about that too."

"Is it because of Thanksgiving?"

She always said anyone who didn't think a nine-year-old knew what was going on in a home should think again. And Jason was proving her point. "That's part of it."

"And 'cause he doesn't like to talk about my mom?"

Now even she was surprised. He seemed to have a better grasp of the situation than his father did. "Yes, I guess that too," she said. "Now you'd better hurry or you'll miss your bus."

"Okay." He struggled to zip his coat.

She stood to help him with the stubborn zipper, then tousled the shock of red hair. "Better put on your hood. It's cold out."

"Okay."

She felt so sorry for him as he stood, dejected, his head down. She was reminded just then of the first day he had come into her classroom. "It'll be all right. You can come in and talk whenever you want."

"Okay, but it's not gonna be the same," he sulked as he turned and shuffled out of the room.

Becky Spooner looked up from her book as Jason came through the door. "Why, hello, young man. How was school?"

"Okay, I guess."

"Not a good one today?"

"It was okay." He went through the gallery and up the stairs at the back. Marc was upstairs working. He had learned to gauge his son's mood by the way he climbed those stairs. Two at a time—it had been a good day. There had been a lot of those lately. Not today though. Today, Marc heard every step echo throughout the gallery. He turned on his stool to watch the boy come into sight. He was wearing a look to match the clumping steps.

"Not a good day, buddy?"

"I'm not in Miss DeLaney's class anymore," he said in little more than a mumble.

Marc's look went from one of amusement at his son's school-day mood to one of real concern. "What happened?"

"I got moved to old Mr. Slama's room."

"But why?"

"I don't know." Jason looked at his father for the first time, his mouth and eyes showing the start of a good pout. "How come you and Miss DeLaney are mad at each other?"

"Did she say that?"

"Sorta."

Marc looked toward the ceiling and gritted his teeth. *I can't believe she would take it out on him. Removing him from her class, of all things.* He met his son's eyes. "We just had a little talk and decided it would be better if we stopped seeing each other for a while."

"Does that mean you don't like her anymore?"

"It doesn't mean that at all. I still like her a lot." He hadn't meant to tell his son so much, but the words had slipped out.

"Then why don't you want to see her?"

"It's kind of complicated. Sometimes things don't always work out the way we want them to."

" 'Cause of Mom?"

Marc looked surprised. "What makes you say that?"

" 'Cause anytime anybody mentions her you get all funny actin'."

Suddenly Marc reached out and pulled Jason close. "I'm sorry about that, buddy. I promise I won't do it again, and we're going to have some long talks about your mom, starting tonight."

"Know what, Dad?"

Marc, his eyes stinging with tears, looked down at the boy. "What?"

''Mom wouldn't mind havin' somebody take care of us, would she?''

Marc hugged him again so he wouldn't see the tears. ''No, I don't suppose she would.'' He held his son tight then, wondering what he ever would have done without him. He let him go after a moment. ''So how about a snack? You hungry?''

''No,'' Jason answered as he peeled off his heavy coat. ''I'd like a can of pop, though.''

Marc fished in his pocket for change. ''Run down to Clancy's and get something.'' He began to put his paints away. ''I'm going over to school to see what's going on.''

Jason turned in alarm. ''Dad, don't!''

Marc stopped his work and looked up. ''Why not?''

''Just 'cause.''

''Just 'cause why?''

'' 'Cause everybody's gonna think I'm a geek, like last year.''

''Nobody's going to think you're a geek.''

''Yes, they will. Please, Dad, don't go.''

''Well, we'll let it slide for a few days, but if there's any trouble, I won't stand for it.''

Chapter Twenty-four

"You're sure he requested the change?" Heather and Shirley were on their way home, and Heather had just told her roommate about Jason's sudden transfer.

"What else could it be?"

Shirley gave her head a little tilt as she watched her friend behind the wheel. "I don't know. I've seen some strange things happen around the old brain factory. Why don't you give him a call?"

Heather glanced over at her. "What on earth for?"

"Clear the air, maybe."

"I assure you the air's already been cleared. That's what brought all this on in the first place. He just found a way he could have the last word, that's all."

Shirley knew that tone. She understood the subject was closed.

Heather looked for Jason to stop in before school, but there was no sign of him. She even sneaked next door while her parent aide was monitoring reading time and saw him at his place in Mr. Slama's room, as attentive as always. She stood at her door after school but again, no Jason. She tried to work at her desk, but she couldn't get him out of her mind. She had a vague feeling of worry. She hadn't liked the mood he was in after school yesterday. She hoped Marc had talked things out with him, something he should have done before he requested a change in the first place. She still couldn't believe the stupidity of such a change in the middle of the school year.

It was about four o'clock, and she had just finished grading the last of the day's spelling quizzes. She yawned and reached for her science workbook to plan tomorrow's lesson.

"Have you seen him?"

Heather jerked her head toward the door. Marc was standing there, one hand on each side of the door frame as if for support. She hadn't recognized his voice, it sounded so strained and harsh. "Who?" she asked.

"Jason!" he practically shouted. "Was he with you?"

She was already on her feet. "No! I haven't seen him all day." Her vague sense of worry now took center stage.

"He didn't show up at the gallery. They're paging the bus driver right now in the office. I came here because I thought he might have been with you."

"Let's check with Mr. Slama." She led him down the hall to Jason's new room, but the door was locked. "He's left for the day," she said. "They should know something in the office by now." The two made their way to the office, the only sound their footsteps echoing off the tile in the hollow halls. The scene there was one of chaos. Two secretaries were waiting by a telephone ready to pounce if the thing made a sound. Miss Nordway was pacing between the desks.

"Well?" he demanded.

"Nothing yet, Mr. Adams," the principal said. "We're waiting for a call from the transportation office. They're contacting the driver by two-way radio."

"If anything has happened to my boy, I'll, I'll . . ."

The ringing of the phone kept him from completing his threat. One of the secretaries grabbed the phone while it was still ringing. "Hello . . . Yes . . . Could you repeat that, please? . . . And he's already off the bus? . . . Tell the driver to keep the note. Thank you.

The secretary turned to face four sets of eyes boring into her. "They contacted the driver, and he said your boy gave him a note signed by you, sir, directing the driver to take him home instead of his regular drop-off spot."

Heather and Marc exchanged glances. "And he's all right?" he demanded.

"Apparently so, sir. He already got off the bus at your house."

Miss Nordway let out a visible sigh of relief. "All's well that ends well."

Marc turned to glare at Heather. "I don't know what got into his head, but whatever it is, it's your fault."

"My fault!" she exploded. "How, may I ask, do you figure that?"

"You're the one who had him taken out of your class. Just because you were mad at me."

Heather was oblivious of the audience of listeners. "Now wait just one minute here. I had nothing to do with his transfer. I thought you were the one who had him moved."

"I certainly did not. Who said that, anyway?" he demanded.

"I guess I just assumed it," Heather said, her voice suddenly much softer. "If not you, then who?" They both turned as if on cue to stare at Miss Nordway.

She was rooted to her spot between the desks, wringing her hands. "I, ah, I mean I thought it was best for the boy. I mean, under the circumstances and all."

"Under what circumstances?" Heather asked, her face registering her total shock.

"You two were, were, you know, romantically involved, and I didn't think it was proper to leave him in your classroom."

Just the start of a giggle escaped one of the secretaries, and she clamped a hand over her mouth as all eyes turned toward her. Her neck and face blushed red. "Excuse me," she said in a strange voice.

"Miss Nordway," Heather said evenly, "I think you might have talked to us before you did anything like that."

"Perhaps in retrospect that would have been a better idea," Miss Nordway said, almost contritely. "At the time it seemed the wisest course."

No one spoke for what seemed minutes, but in thinking back, Heather realized it couldn't have been longer than seconds. Finally Marc cleared his throat. He was both relieved and a little embarrassed by what had just happened. Sure, he wasn't pleased with Miss Nordway's tampering, but, after all, it was his boy who had scared them all with a forged note. "I'm sorry about all this. I'd better get home and talk it over with him. Miss Nordway, maybe we could get together in the next day or so about what's best for the boy. He was doing very well with Miss DeLaney.''

She nodded. ''I'm aware of that. I'd be glad to talk things over. Maybe I was a little hasty.''

''Let me get my coat, and I'll go with you,'' Heather said.

One of the secretaries was looking frantically through the papers on her desk. ''Oh, Miss DeLaney, just a minute. I almost forgot. A student gave me a note to put in your mailbox, and I forgot about it with all the hubbub around here after school. It's here someplace. Yes, here it is.'' She handed over the note, a piece of typing paper folded once. Heather opened it and glanced at the typewritten contents as she turned to go back to her room. She stopped in her tracks.

''Marc, look at this.'' He stepped closer and read over her shoulder.

Dear Miss DeLaney,

You like my dad a lot and he does you too. Why can't you come to my house to visit him like before? I am going to the mountain to live for a month or maybe two. Then maybe you will come take care of my dad.

Your Freind
Jason Adams

Heather fought to keep the panic out of her voice. ''Marc, we've got to stop him before he leaves the house.''

Their eyes met. ''Let's go!'' he shouted and sprinted down the hall to the side-door opening to the parking lot, with Heather right on his heels. Once she stepped out the door the late November chill cut through Heather's light sweater, but she hardly noticed. When she climbed into the car, though, she began to shake uncontrollably, whether from the cold or from her fear for Jason she couldn't tell. Marc started the car and slammed it into gear. He glanced across at her. ''You're shaking. We forgot your coat. You must be freezing.''

''Don't worry about me. Just drive!''

And Marc drove as he'd never driven before. They said nothing except once when Heather put a hand on his arm and shouted a warning about a car pulling onto the main highway from a mountain road. The drive took no more than fifteen minutes, but those were the longest fifteen minutes Heather had ever endured. They both saw the house at the same time, lights clearly visible in several windows. The lights raised their hopes, but also reminded them that it was already getting dark outside. "He wouldn't go out in the dark, would he?" Heather asked, and was surprised that she had spoken the words out loud.

"I hope not. Oh, how I hope not," Marc said. He slammed on the brakes in front of the garage and the two sprang from the car. The front door was unlocked, and Marc burst in, Heather close behind. "Jason!" he shouted. "Jason! Are you here?" There was no answer except for the barking of the dog in the garage, hoping it was time to come out for the evening. They hurried from room to room downstairs, then did the same upstairs, but there was no sign of the boy. They returned to the main floor, and Marc went straight for the phone in the kitchen. "I'm going to call for help." As he picked up the phone, he spotted a note resting on the kitchen table. He hung up the phone and snatched up the note. Done on the computer, it was similar to the one Heather had gotten at school.

Dear Dad,

Don't worry. I am real warm with my sleeping bag. I took peanut butter for two months. I took your good flashlight. Sorry. Don't be mad at me and tell Miss DeLaney not to be mad too.

Love,
Jason

Heather felt the tears well, and she put an arm on Marc's shoulder. She felt him shudder at the touch. His head bowed. "I've *got* to call the sheriff. We've got to start a search before it gets any darker. It's cold out there, and it's going to get a lot colder."

She could hear the panic in his voice, and she could also hear Smoky still barking for attention in the garage. Strange, she thought. Why would a boy go off on an adventure like this without his dog? At that moment an idea crept into her brain. It was a wild, crazy, absurd idea, but just the kind she wouldn't put past a nine-year-old. *And who,* she said to herself, *knows nine-year-old ideas better than a fourth-grade teacher?* Marc had the telephone to his ear again and was preparing to dial. "Wait," she said as she put a hand on the receiver.

He looked at her, wild eyed. "Are you crazy? We're wasting time. Jason's out there someplace." He waved his hand toward the window.

"Maybe not."

"What do you mean?"

"Do you know the story of Anne Frank?"

"The girl who wrote about hiding from the Nazis? Sure. What's that got to do with anything?"

"Jason knows about it too. We had a lesson on part of her diary just last week."

Marc looked at her as if she had taken leave of her senses. His face was tense with worry. Suddenly his eyes came alive as Heather's idea struck him. "And you think . . ."

"That Jason might be hiding right here in the house," she finished for him.

"But why?"

"I think that's obvious."

His eyebrows arched. "You mean the two of us?" He pointed from one to the other.

"Exactly," she said slowly, as if she were explaining a math assignment to one of her students. "Now let's find out if he was paying as much attention in class as I think he was."

"I only hope you're right. If not, we're wasting valuable time. You look down here, and I'll go upstairs."

"Wait, I've got a better idea. Let's get Smoky."

Marc hurried to the door leading to the garage and let the excited dog into the house. He circled the pair, barking his happiness at winning his freedom. Marc dropped to his haunches by the dog and took the big head in his arms. "Smoky, find Jason. Come on, boy, find Jason."

The big lab raced through the living room and into the kitchen. Next, he made a turn through the family room and then bolted down the hall toward the solarium, where his barking brought Heather and Marc on the run. They found him whining in front of the louvered doors of a closet that stretched across one whole side of the room. Heather saw the doors vibrate ever so slightly. "Good dog," she whispered as she patted the big dog's head.

Marc pulled both doors open with one quick yank to reveal Jason wrapped in his sleeping bag, a set of headphones on his ears, surrounded by the peanut butter jar, a whole loaf of bread, crackers, cookies, cans of pop, and the flashlight. He shielded his eyes against the light and looked up at the pair, a weak smile on his face. "Hi, Dad."

Marc stood with his hands on his hips, his relief and happiness at finding the boy at war with his anger at what he and Heather had just been put through. His sense of relief easily won out. "Come here," he commanded.

Jason climbed out of the closet dutifully, knowing that tone of voice. But his own worry that maybe he had gone too far with his little trick quickly dissolved as his dad wrapped him in a big bear hug. "Do you know how worried you had us?" Marc said, his voice husky with emotion.

"I'm sorry, Dad."

"Well, I hope so." Marc held him at arm's length so he could look at him. "Why did you ever do such a thing?"

" 'Cause I wanted you and Miss DeLaney to like each other again."

Marc glanced at Heather, who was not even trying to hide her tears. He took her hand. "Well, that was a mighty strange way to do it," he said.

Jason, feeling more confident with himself with each passing minute, cocked his head to one side and smirked. "It worked, didn't it?"

Marc pulled the boy close again and put a playful headlock on him. "Why, you little rascal! You're getting too clever with that computer. I think maybe we'll turn off the Death Rockets for a couple of weeks."

"Dad!" the boy whined as he wriggled free and retreated back to the closet with Smoky right behind him. "I won't do it again, ever. I promise."

Marc smiled down at him. "I should hope not." He was still

holding Heather's hand, and he squeezed it gently as he looked at her. "How come you're so quiet?"

"I don't know what to say. I'm just too happy."

"Is there anything you don't know about fourth graders?"

She gave a little laugh. "Want to know the truth? I learn something new about them every day."

"Well, you've got this one all figured out." He nodded at Jason, who was busy trying to squeeze Smoky into the sleeping bag. "See all the trouble you caused by dumping me?"

Though he was trying to hide it, she could see the beginning of a smile around his eyes. She couldn't help laughing. "I didn't dump you."

"Yes, you did. Not that I blame you." With a quick motion he closed both louvered doors on Jason again. He had to push a wagging tail inside before he got the second door shut.

"Hey!" the boy exclaimed in surprise, but the doors stayed closed.

He took her hand again. "I had some things to tell you last Friday, but I didn't get around to them. A certain someone didn't give me a chance. But better late than never." He took a deep breath and plunged ahead. "I did a lot of thinking last Thursday night. In fact, I didn't sleep much at all that night."

Heather nodded. "Welcome to the club."

He went on. "I finally learned some things about myself. I figured out, before you even told me on Friday, that I'd been living in the past. Well, not anymore, I promise you. Now don't get me wrong. I have no intention of erasing the past. I can talk about it, but I want to *live* for the future." He squeezed her hand. "And I want to live that future with you, if you'll let me." He studied her for a reaction.

She stared back, trying to convince herself that she had really heard those words. Apparently she waited too long, because she saw his eyes cloud with doubt and had to rush to reassure him. "Yes," she said with a nod of her head, and her words came almost in a whisper. "I want that too. More than anything in the world."

Those were the words he had been so afraid to hope for. He pulled her to him before she could change her mind and found her lips with his own. This was the kiss she had been waiting for, the kiss she was afraid he would never be able to share.

"Yuck!" It was Jason from inside the closet. He had been watching them through the louvers. They pulled away from each other in embarrassment at his one-word critique.

"Jason," Marc said, "you weren't supposed to be watching."

"You're gonna get girl germs," was the response from inside the closet.

"Hey, young man, just remember that in another six years or so." He took Heather by the hand. "Just ignore him. What does he know?" He led her away from the closet. "I've got an early Christmas present for you. I was afraid I wasn't going to be able to give it to you." He took her toward the easel still standing near the wall of windows, where it had been that night when he snapped at her for threatening to uncover the painting on it. The canvas was still there as before. "Go ahead, uncover it."

She looked at him with arched eyebrows. "Are you sure?"

"I'm more than sure."

She lifted the material carefully and pulled it free of the canvas, and inhaled sharply at the beauty of what was unveiled before her. "Marc, it's lovely."

"It's yours. I did it for you. I was able to finish it because of you. You don't know how close I came to destroying it the other night when I thought I'd lost you. I'm just glad I didn't."

"Oh, Marc, I'm glad you didn't either. It's so beautiful."

"When I was a little boy, a little younger than Jason, I used to help my grandmother pick the biggest, reddest apples in that orchard. We used to sit right there when we were through." He pointed to a small bench tucked between two of the trees. "Right there. She used to tell me stories as we sat there together about when she was a little girl, or sometimes made-up ones that went on and on. She was a wonderful storyteller." He looked so deeply into the painting it was as if he had gone back to that time, if only for a second. "I always felt so secure, so at peace, so loved when I was in that place." Now his words became difficult and his voice husky. "Heather, when I think of that feeling, I think of you."

"Thank you," she murmured as she buried her head in his chest.

"Are you gonna kiss her again?" Jason called from behind the louvered doors.

The two looked at each other. "I swear." Marc groaned. "That kid is incorrigible. Do you think you can put up with the two of us?"

"I'd like to try," she said with a smile.

He pulled her close. "You know, I have to admit, sometimes he has some pretty good ideas," he said as his lips found hers again.